THE HEPHAESTUS PLAGUE

THE HEPHAESTUS PLAGUE

PLAGUE

Thomas Page

G. P. Putnam's Sons, New York

To JAMES T. JORDAN
and the memory of the sandhills.

Part 1

SUMMER, EARLY FALL

August 12

IN the great empty stretch of sand and sky sat the tiny, one-story, white clapboard Baptist church. Within it resided one aged wooden organ and the Reverend Dan C. Potter, a sixty-seven-year-old local boy who had been called by the Lord at the age of fifty-one after miraculously surviving a heart attack down at the peach canning plant.

Dan had a special treat for his flock that night. The Reverend Kern Speece of Beulah Hill Baptist Church, down near Southern Pines, was coming over to turn loose one of his sulfurous forty-five-minute jobs, after which cakes and lemonade would be served in the vestry.

Pickups, flatbeds, and tractors lined the one-lane road before the church that lazy evening. Henry Tacker came late and parked his John Deere with the plow raised under the trees. His wife, Ruth, had taken the Ford earlier that afternoon to deliver a bowl of potato salad to the church.

Since Henry was the last to arrive, he had to stand in the sweaty, gasping heat behind the last pew. Reverend Speece, a short, grinning man in a shiny green suit, was just warming up as Henry silently closed the door.

"Brothers," intoned the Reverend, "first off, when you go home, I want you to get out a map of these United States—an Esso one will do—and trace out the path of hell scything through this nation. Our cities are in pain and turmoil, the pestilence of Babylon is everywhere! Just take a little red pencil and mark your map where you've read of a riot or a murder or a rape. The courage and basic goodness of our lovely sun-washed land is awash with the flowing boils"—Speece pronounced this last as "berls"—"of the devil's own excrement."

"Amen," whispered Rose Flinger of Route 5. Rose had recently become a widow, when a falling cinder block had killed her husband, Frank Jack Flinger, leaving her the Grain and Feed Store.

Speece loosened his thin tie, stepped away from the podium, and mopped his face with a bandanna. "Two hundred years of accumulating virtue, my friends, lie quivering under the lashes of sin. There is confusion and despair in this country, the blood of Christ mingles with the hate and rage. The women of the land are sacrifices on the altar of lust, their clean, fair, pure flesh—*flesh*, I say!—the vessel of your damnable spurting fountains of noisome mortality. They ask if God is dead! Well, every time you folks get a check from the canning plant or the warehouse, you get a kiss from God. That *such* a question should even be *asked*—in the North—is an indication of how far from God's gentle caress the hairy heads of our children have wandered."

"Amen," said Ruth Tacker sternly winking back at Henry.

"Amen!" blurted Henry who was missing the Frank Sinatra special on Channel 4 this very minute.

Speece removed his coat and took a sip of ice water. His voice foamed and poured forth like a surging river swelling against the church walls. "You and me and all of us is just dangling over a yawning pit of boiling teeth, *Satan*'s teeth. Now I know it sounds kind of, well, *funny* for me to stand here and say God's gonna fry your soul, on the one hand, and he loves you, on the other, but darn it, God is just like you and me. We are in His image! When He made this here universe you can *bet* He didn't let us in on every little ole thing He put down here 'cause His wonders exceed just about everything you could ever imagine even when *drunk*!" Speece's finger jabbed out now at the rapt faces opening to his words. "Oh, yeah, God is there, and He is gettin' madder by the minute! God is comin' up with some trick to remind us that while He might still love us, He is still the boss and we ain't behavin' ourselves. . . ."

The flow of Speece's voice slowly disappeared beneath the low, throaty, earthen rumble that welled up through the floorboards of the church, vibrating the spines of the parishioners, climbing the walls and cracking the windows. A heavy wood beam shook loose and crashed down to within inches of Speece's head. Shouts of panic mingled with the roar as the church's very underpinnings trembled, knocking dust loose from thousands of cracks and sending it floating into the air.

An earthquake had hit Montgomery County.

As the waves of thunder subsided, Henry Tacker, still closest to the door, flung it open and looked out to see the little grove of trees shaking in the moonlight. The babble of voices was solidly pierced by Speece's voice. "Now calm down, folks, just calm down."

Dan Potter's bellow stilled the panicky rush of feet into the aisles. "It's over, folks, stop it now! Henry, run on over to the telephone and call Harry Shaw at the radio station and find out what's happening. The rest of you folks head for the vestry. The food's waitin'!"

Ten minutes later Tacker returned. "Harry was in bed," he announced. "He looked around and called up some people who said it was an earthquake. There ain't any damage yet according to the fire department, so what the hell! Sorry, Reverends!"

There was a burst of nervous laughter and the lines reformed for the food. Ruth brought her husband a heavily laden paper plate full of chicken and salad. "Henry, I bet the Army was testing some bombs again"—she pronounced the word "bums"—" 'Member when they had them maneuvers down here six years ago?"

"Shut up, Ruth, and gimme one of them apples there."

Hank Prince and Harmon Shull from the Volunteer Fire Department dropped in and were given some cookies. "Busted up Frank Stone's curing house, but that's about all though. We went down there when the quake went off but wasn't no other calls or nothin'."

At one o'clock Reverend Speece delivered a benediction to the guests, who bowed their heads and assumed a silence in the back of the church broken only by the drunken giggles of Sam and Harry Westbrook, who had been hitting a little Southern Comfort from a pint bottle in a brown paper bag.

Henry Tacker drove the tractor home just behind Ruth in the Ford. They stopped at the bumpy gravel drive leading to the tiny house on which they had owed a mortgage ever since they were married. The side of the house was a pile of jumbled slats, twistings of broken lumber, pipe, and broken glass. Stretching off to the invisible horizon was Tacker's five-hundred-acre crescent of north pastureland, pressed flat under the bloated darkness of the summer night. Henry had begun a peach orchard at the northern tip of that land last year. He stared out at the dark, then walked up to his sobbing wife and put his arm around her waist. They looked at the back of the house. Water gurgled from broken pipes thunking against the ruptured lumber of the extra bathroom that Henry had built two years ago for the baby Ruth had miscarried. Henry calculated in silence the cost of raw materials against probable insurance money, while Ruth cried against his shoulder. Far off in the north pasture in the direction of the orchard, Henry heard swarms of crickets, their jagged cries climbing to the starry skies and spreading like clouds of sound across the same heavenly firmament against which they had been warned by Reverend Speece.

They spent the night at the Prince place two miles up the road. In the morning, while Eileen Prince fed Ruth a gigantic breakfast and talked about the gall bladder operation she had had just after their stables had burned years ago, Henry went to examine his house.

Henry Tacker's farm had sustained the worst damage of any in the quake. He drove the John Deere into the north pasture, noticing how the sandy ground now bore concentric rings that increased in depth the closer he got to the orchard. The rings, or ridges, formed a rough bowl, the center of which was a row of toppled and uprooted peach trees slicing through the orchard corner in a perfect north–south diagonal line. The line formed the locus of the quake, and here a raw gash lay open in the ground, bridged in places by shattered tree trunks. Henry guessed the chasm was more than thirty feet long and nine feet deep at most. Sand had poured in after the quake, so there was no telling whether the ground had fractured all of the hundred feet down to the bedrock.

Henry stepped out on the trunk of one of the trees he had so carefully pruned last year and peered into the chasm. He saw only sand and gap-toothed rocks. Inside a tangle of branches jammed into the chasm, though, Henry quite clearly heard the chatter of crickets.

August 13

THE man with the explosion of white hair was obviously uncomfortable with Montgomery County and everything in it. He chose his words carefully, for he realized that Henry Tacker's vocabulary was limited. "It's in Washington. The Smithsonian."

Over his spectacles Henry read the sheet of paper before him. "The Institute of Short-Lived Phenomena."

"We recorded the quake on a seismograph last night and came as fast as we could."

Henry blinked at the man. "Why?"

"To examine the site."

"They ain't nothin' out there. Just a ditch."

"The quake recorded two-oh-five on the Richter Scale. That's the seismograph recording of it in your hand."

"You mean these little squiggles and lines here."

"That's right. There weren't any aftershocks, which is kind of unusual. And since it was so mild, the lock fault is pretty deep. It's probably been under pressure for a couple of thousand years."

"You don't say. Couple thousand years!" Henry looked at the jumble of timber that had once been his home. "That's real nice of it to go off just when I got my trees planted. A thousand years ago I wasn't livin' here. It couldn't go off then! The fucker had to wait till I got set up, *then* cut loose!" Tacker folded up the paper and handed it to the geologist. "I'll take you out there, but I got to come right back here and clear this up and check out the insurance so if. . . ."

"Oh, you'll find us quite vigorous, Mr. Tacker." The white-haired man laughed. "We go all over the world. Last year I was in Iceland checking out a volcano."

"That a fact?" Henry trudged into the field, the white-haired man just behind him and two others just behind him.

"We're used to exercise."

One of the men passed out from the heat in the middle of the

13

field, and Tacker gripped one of his arms around his shoulder and hoisted him to his feet. "This feller here wasn't in Iceland I'll bet?"

The white-haired man looked ahead at the gap shimmering like a mirage. Children were playing in it, clambering through the orchard branches and making little games of microcosmic war with sandy cliffs that collapsed so beautifully. "Them kids won't bother you. Just take your measurements and your pictures and everything and come on back to the house for some food when you're finished. Although there ain't much house left."

The scientists were back ten minutes after Tacker had left them. The white-haired man said, "I've never felt heat like that."

"Yeah?" Henry and Harmon Shull and Jordy Harris were clearing away wreckage.

"We got what we came for, though. I saw those children playing with some black stones, Mr. Tacker. Any idea what they were?"

"Nope."

"They wouldn't let me see any."

"Little brats, hey?"

"Oh, well, I guess we'll be moving along. Let us know if you want any information on earthquakes. Just call me collect."

Tacker paused with his load of lumber. With great control, he refrained from braining the geologists with it. "Just as soon as I can, mister, I'll ask you all about earthquakes. But I'm kinda busy now." And he remained busy for the rest of the week working deep into the velvet evenings when the only light came from the undamaged porch. The yellow light under which he labored attracted hundreds of swooping moths and gnats and Henry stopped work only when Ruth, her hair in curlers, shouted up to him that it was ten thirty.

Henry did not even try to clear the orchard. He got a line of credit and insurance and concentrated his efforts on stacking the pipe and lumber delivered to his yard. He wanted to rebuild the house himself, so he sent Harmon and Jordy away and worked alone. Nine hours a day.

IT was brutally hot that Friday afternoon when Jordy Harris' seven-year-old son Herman came over to play alone in Tacker's chasm. The child parked his bike against the side of the house and wandered out into the dazzlingly bright fields with his arms full of plastic Sherman tanks, a jeep, and a steam shovel.

Henry was sitting on a slanting beam twenty-five feet above ground, a nail clenched in his lips and a hammer in his hand, when a child's scream of terror and pain, thin and high, floated delicately over the hot, still air from the orchard. Henry lowered his hammer and squinted through the shimmering yellow haze at Herman's tiny figure wavering in the heat, running hell for leather toward the house with his right hand held out. Still screaming, the boy disappeared into the kitchen and Ruth's arms.

Henry, glad of any excuse to get indoors out of the heat, found Herman at the kitchen table with a huge glass of chocolate milk. Ruth was wrapping ice in a rag at the sink. The boy squalled as Henry grabbed his hand and looked at the injury. In the center of Herman's right hand was a huge, fluidy blister.

"Goddammit Herman," snarled Henry, softening his words by laying his other hand on the boy's shoulder, "be a man!"

"I ain't cryin'."

"I know you ain't. What'd you do to your hand anyhow."

"Bug burned it."

"Say that ag'in?"

Ruth tied the ice rag around Herman's hand. "Henry, quit pickin' on him. I'm callin' the doctor."

"He don't need no doctor," Henry said.

"I don't need no doctor!" Herman said.

Doc Travis' seven-year-old Cadillac was the most expensive car in seven square miles. He parked it in the dirt, slapped the cloud of dust from his gray pants, and walked into Tacker's kitchen with his bag.

After releasing Herman's hand, Travis removed his glasses and pursed his lips. "Now, Herman, where did you get those matches?"

"I ain't got no matches! I picked up a beetle, and he burned me sure enough!"

Henry growled, "You gonna say that to your daddy, Herman?"

"Sure am!" the boy cried defiantly.

Travis pulled from his bag a cotton bandage and a thicker pair of glasses. He peered closely again at Herman's swollen hand. Ruth said hesitantly, "Edgar, I called because I was afraid a snake or something got him."

"This is a blister all right."

Herman's lip quivered. "It don't hurt no more." Travis' interest presaged something mysterious, possibly even a needle.

"That's a burn okay, Herman."

Herman sobbed once.

Tacker shouted, "Shut your mouth, Herman, and be still! Goddammit all to hell!"

Herman choked out between sobs, "My momma . . . told . . . me that swearing was . . . bad . . . Mr. Tacker."

"Shit!" Tacker bellowed.

Travis took out a long, slender, silver probe. Herman tried to pull his hand away. "You gonna pop it open?"

Travis held Herman's hand and traced the probe around the edges of the blister, narrowing his path until he came to rest against a tiny blackened sore in the center of the burn. "There's a cut of some kind in the middle here."

"Bug did it."

Travis removed his glasses and glared at Herman. "Insect? You sure, Herman?"

"I picked it up. That's how it happened. God's truth!"

"What kind of bug?"

"Looked like a tiger beetle, sounded like a cricket!"

"Tiger beetles don't burn folks, Herman. No bug I ever heard of does."

"This one did."

Ruth asked, "Where'd you find him, Herman?"

"Out there in that hole, ma'am, on one of Mr. Tacker's peach trees."

Henry said, "Herman, there ain't nothing like that in my orchard because Henry McPartland sprayed it last spring."

Herman crossed his arms and adamantly replied, "Mary Louise Ketcher and Frannie Peters all saw a couple when they come out here Wednesday. You look at your peach trees, that's all I have to say."

Tacker raged out of his chair, bearing down on Herman, clenched fist quivering before the boy's nose. "Ain't no Goddamn bugs on my peach trees, Herman."

"Is too! Is too!"

Travis dropped his metal probe in surprise at Henry's fury.

"Godalmighty, Henry, he's just a boy!" Ruth cried.

Henry's face was purple and splotchy white above his beet-red neck. "I'm gonna burn the hide off that boy if he keeps talkin' like that! I take care of my peach trees, Herman; you just shut up about them!"

Herman started crying again.

Ruth cried, "Quit pickin' on him, Henry!"

"You shut up, too!" Henry turned on her. Depths of rage and frustration Ruth had never seen before in Henry had been unsluiced by the loss of the orchard. He jabbed his finger at Herman's tear-streaked face. "I planted that orchard, I took care of them trees, and there ain't no bugs of no kind out there, y'hear? I spent my life learnin' peaches—you think I'd let a bug in there? It's as clean out there as a damn hospital. So, Herman, you just shut up this shit right this minute now!"

Tacker's last words were shouted through the banging screen door at Herman's running figure. Herman vaulted onto his bike, still crying, and peddled frantically down the gravel drive. Tacker shouted at the boy's retreating figure. "I catch you lying again, Herman, I'm gonna bust your face off!" Then Tacker sat down slowly and avoided their eyes.

Travis said, "Henry? Herman isn't a liar. That boy was burned."

Tacker took a deep sad breath and stared out the window.

Travis continued, "Henry, what say we just duck on down to the orchard and look around?"

Tacker did small things with his fingers, turning a fork over on the table and scraping under his nails. He breathed very deeply and regularly. "Shit, I musta scared poor Herman half to death."

"What do you say, Henry?"

"You go on home, Doc, I'll check."

"I'd be glad to . . . ."

"Go on home, Doc."

Travis stood. He slapped Henry's shoulder. "Kids!" he said. Henry did not answer; he scraped at the tablecloth, so Travis bowed to Ruth and left.

Ruth said to Henry, "Hungry?"

"Hell, no. Got any ham left?"

"Sure."

"Never mind. Could I have some cheddar with it?"

"I'll fix it right now."

"I ain't hungry."

"Remind me to call Jordy and get that rag back."

"How'n hell am I gonna lay pipes into the wing in fall?"

"I've run out of combats, by the way, and my period's on Saturday."

The conversation between Henry and his wife would have sounded surrealistic to an outsider but was perfectly understandable to any couple who had lived together as long as they had.

Henry wolfed down three ham and cheese sandwiches.

Ruth asked, "You gonna check the orchard?"

"Ain't no bugs on my peach trees!" Henry growled.

He wearily climbed up the house frame, and his nail hammering and grumbled curses filled the rest of the dusty golden afternoon.

August 18

WITHIN the cavernous expanses of Jordy Harris' Blue Ribbon Tobacco warehouse lay piles of green cured leaf on sheets of fibrous cloth. More than a hundred farmers, buyers, drivers, rustled through the heat-baked dimness as the auctioneer's trilling, syllabic incantations reverberated through the booming space.

The farmers had been arriving to stack their leaf since seven in the morning. Yesterday had brought good prices, the best in three years, and Jordy Harris had turned away several farmers who had arrived too late to find space on the floor. The selling began at nine and the shadowy interior had been alive with activity ever since.

By ten the Coke machines were empty and bottles were rolling around the floor. Jordy followed the company buyers down each aisle tagging the leaf and was, in turn, followed by farmers and office girls with clipboards. Henry Tacker dropped by for a bit of human company. Solomon Burgess and the Tucker cousins traded crop stories with him while Frank Flynn drove off into Candor and returned with a six pack.

When the trucks started moving out at eleven for distant—by Southern standards—towns like Lynchburg or Richmond, Petersburg, Greensboro or Durham or Raleigh and Winston-Salem, Jordy was dashing over to the wall phone and making quick calls. "Come on in Wednesday, Sam, we'll be goin' at two . . . pretty damn good . . . pretty *damn* good, in fact. . . ."

Under the heady buzz of the beer and the rapid-fire talk of the others, Henry Tacker began to feel a little better. He smiled slightly and opened another beer. Then he looked over at an elfin figure in jeans sniffing at the pungent leaf and bellowed, "What's the matter, Herman, lookin' for ticks?"

Herman dodged a gentle kick from Jordy Harris and scooted under a table. His wide eyes stared up at the towering legs shuffling by. He rested his chin in his hands, drinking in the noise and the crowd and the voices that dealed and calculated. Backing out from under the table carried him between the legs of a group of aged farmers on stools seated in the aisle. One of them grabbed him by the seat of the pants and hauled him upright. The farmer chortled. "We got us here a little chigger!"

Herman squirmed under the leathery taloned hand. "Afternoon, Mr. Person. That hurts!"

The farmer ruffled his hair. "Don't you go messin' up any of that Gold over there or your daddy will whap you. What you lookin' for anyhow?"

"I seen a bug in here. Big black one!"

"Big chigger, eh?"

"No, sir! Big black thing. They can make fire. I seen them. They can make flames come out of their tail and smoke and sparks and they can outrun a beagle . . . ." Herman went on for a while perfectly seriously until a guffaw and slap on the rear sent him dashing down the aisle again.

At two o'clock the last truck was being loaded by men streaming on the concrete ramp that blazed white under the sun. A small knot of jubilant farmers squinted out at the truck and the shimmering fields across the road in which Jordy Harris' wooden house squatted.

Herman Harris could not stop talking even though the farmers did not listen to him. ". . . an' these bugs can fly faster than an F-4 Phantom an' when they go they make this . . . whoooo. . . ."

Herman was cut off with a squawk as Jordy grabbed his son by the suspenders and yanked him off the floor. Herman swung at his father, who held him out at arm's length. Presently Jordy said, "Okay, Herman, go home and tell your mommer I'm comin' in at four. Scat!" Jordy dropped the boy off the edge of the warehouse platform.

Herman said, "Yessir" and took off across the road.

As Jordy Harris lit a huge cigar, he said, "You all should get your checks after the next weekend. Ever'body satisfied?"

The farmers shuffled and nodded. One of them spat onto the concrete.

The truck roared, creaked its brakes loose and, with a clank and thunder, began easing out of the loading ramp onto the road. There was a sudden thunderous backfire that cracked across the fields. The truck stalled.

Jordy and the others shouted advice. "Kill the throttle . . . open the throttle. . . . It's a little dry there . . . easy now . . . easy. . . ."

The truck's ignition whined. The engine caught, died, then caught again and roared loudly. It rumbled onto the road and off into the distance, leaving a small clatter of tiny black stones from beneath the chassis on the road.

A farmer said, "Herman's right about them bugs. They say they're all over the place."

"You seen any?" Jordy snapped.

"No, but I know lots of people who have. You know the Gilbert place over in Troy? Well, I heard that two nights ago at midnight, real dark y' know, no moon or nothin', this salesman saw some."

"What was a salesman doing at that old place?"

The farmer's eyes widened between wrinkles of flesh. He gestured with his hands. "His car broke down, see? And there he is all alone at night when he hears somethin' inside the house an' he goes in. . . ."

"And?"

"Well, I hear he was checked into the mental hospital at Butner. His hair was white and he weighed fifty-two pounds, and whatever he saw. . . ."

"Shit!" bellowed Jordy.

"He's gonna be there for the rest of his life. He can't talk or think or make sense or *nothin'*! He's been scared out of his mind."

"Shit!" Jordy repeated.

Another farmer said, "That Gilbert place is bad now. . . ."

The group broke up and left for home.

Jordy checked to see all the sales were entered correctly on the clipboards and started for home. At the loading ramp he paused and looked down at the black stones that had fallen out of the tobacco truck. He kicked one into the scrubby grass and walked on.

When Jordy Harris' figure was a shimmering speck in the distance, the black stones simultaneously unfolded thin multiple legs from beneath their hulks. Quietly they hoisted themselves up. Antennae unrolled to caress the air. Quietly they crawled across the concrete into the grass bordering the warehouse. And waited.

At three in the morning some terror more primeval than a dream awoke Ruth Tacker. She sat bolt upright in the bedroom, drenched in terror-sweat, hearing the crickets and feeling the heavy moon through the window. "Henry! Git up!" she gasped, as she kicked him savagely in the hip.

Henry was up and on the floor, pulling overalls over his underwear before asking, "What's up, Sugarpuss?"

"I don't know! Take a look!"

Ruth's instincts were flawless. Nothing less than war would ever have disturbed her sleep.

A double-barreled shotgun with two rounds rested in the shoe closet. Henry danced across the room, pulling on his boots; he grabbed the gun and broke it open to see if the cartridges were fresh.

Ruth slipped on the huge squirrel-shaped, furry bedroom slippers Henry had given her last anniversary. "Henry, you don't need that thing! Check the kitchen window, the back one!"

Henry flung open the kitchen window and heard the flames crackling far out in the north pasture. His night vision stabilized and he saw the dirty orange-red glow of fire lining the horizon, bringing with it on the wind the obscene taste of woodsmoke, from green bark mixed with burning insecticide spray. The broken trees of his peach orchard were burning. A fire had started in the midst of dry sand in the center of the sandhills.

August 19

RUTH watched Henry drive the tractor out toward the orchard. The expression on his face as he sipped his coffee had terrified her. She called Reverend Potter and Doctor Travis.

Henry parked the tractor by the chasm and looked at the hissing ruins of the trees. The air was pungent with smoke. Leaves, buds, roots, and gnarled bark from the trees were now chunky foul-smelling ash.

When Travis and Reverend Potter found him, Henry was still sitting in the tractor, eyes watering from the smoke. Travis looked up at the sun. It was going to be another scorcher. He shook Henry's arm. "Henry, come on. Let's look for the bugs." Light and rage came into Henry's dulled eyes. The rage gathered in intensity as the two men kicked up clouds of wood and sand. Insects.

Something was to blame for the destruction of his crop. Henry felt bloodlust clamp over him and he rained curses onto the sand he churned into the air.

Travis stopped suddenly. He grabbed Henry's arm again. "Listen!" he whispered.

Henry stopped. "Huh?"

"Crickets!"

They had been audible all along, busy little chirps, floating across sun-baked fields. It was such a normal country sound that Travis' mind had rejected them until he remembered crickets should not sing so loudly in the daytime. The orchard must be crawling with them.

There was a great thrashing of boots and gasping, and Reverend Potter's puffing body appeared beside them. He said, "Henry, God is. . . ." Tacker's motion cut him off.

Travis softly stepped up to a burned piece of wood half buried in the sand next to the chasm. He listened intently, head bent forward. Three chirps. It was beneath the wood, and it was not an average, cheerful singing bug. The sounds were too low-pitched, like tearing cloth or chalk scraping across a blackboard, less like singing and more like growling. Travis slipped his toe under the edge of the wood and spread his arms for balance. He flipped the wood aside and they all saw the creature at once.

It was a great, heavy beetle half buried in the sand, easily three inches long, with a bulbous shape, like a thick-armored teardrop. The iridescent carapace was so black in color that it glittered blue and green in the fierce sunlight. A pair of long antennae hoisted up and tasted the air.

Tacker stepped forward and Travis cautioned, "Hold it, Henry, let's just watch a minute."

The bug crawled with obvious difficulty toward another piece of wood, its stiff legs making little swimming motions in the sand. It moved very slowly and painfully, stopping at each obstacle, usually a stone, to examine it with a sweep of its antennae. Then the antennae touched the wood with an audible *clack* that forced an inadvertent "Jesus!" from Henry Tacker.

23

The bug's weight worked against it. It scrabbled clumsily for footholes in the wood and finally clambered to the surface, its antennae moving across the wood like minesweepers.

Henry stepped toward the bug again, and once again Travis halted him. Reverend Potter was unashamedly goggle-eyed. God, he thought, Thy wonders fill the mind.

Travis noted that the section of wood the bug was on was unburned. Before he could mention this, the creature unleashed a screaming, shockingly loud series of chirps that racketed across the sand.

The insect's hindquarters vibrated. Travis saw a pair of tiny cerci—rear antennae—fluttering like hummingbird wings beneath the tail. And from beneath the rear rose a small thin spiral of blue woodsmoke. Then a spark winked and spread. The chirping stopped. The bug backed up until its blunt head lay over the tiny scorch.

When they heard it scraping at the wood, Henry cried, "Godalmighty! Bastard, bastard . . ." and crunched his boot down on the creature, wood and all, grinding it into the sand. "Bastard, bastard, bastard. . . ." When he calmed down, both wood and insect were buried. "Bastard!" Henry said again to the morning.

From the sand came a scraping sound. A pair of antennae sprouted up from the boot-shaped depression and presently the insect welled painfully up to the sun again. Henry's leather boots might just as well have been stomping a rock. With immense dignity the bug began its slow clambering progress through the sand again, looking for another piece of wood with movements so stately that he might have been chiding Henry's lack of respect for some great primal power whose ways were inevitably bound to frustrate and baffle peach farmers.

September 21

"METBAUM?"

"Huh." Metbaum put his guitar down and rolled up the car window so he could hear the professor more clearly.

"I had an idea, Metbaum. Suppose God transferred his covenant from man to the insects. It would explain a lot."

"Yeah?"

"Um. Maybe the next Jesus is a roach."

"Yeah."

"And no piddling crucifixion would stop him. You see, Metbaum, bugs have so many things humans desire. Order. Stability. Endurance. Security. God was good to insects, Metbaum. Think I'll throw that out in class on Monday."

"Like out the window, Doc?"

"How far to Candor, Metbaum?"

Metbaum traced out a blue line on the road map. He grabbed the dash as Parmiter swung the wheel to avoid a tobacco truck pulling out of a side road.

"I guess thirty miles."

"Nice day for hunting beetles."

Metbaum strummed the guitar once. "You'd never be able to prove that theory to any preacher, Doc."

"I could prove a Virgin Birth. There's a strain of Surinam roach consisting entirely of females. They breed only other females. How about that, Metbaum?"

Metbaum considered it, eyes watching the flat fields rush by. "I have to admit," he said, "that I didn't know that."

James Lang Parmiter had once been described by a colleague as a sinister Gandhi. He was short, very thin, with a smooth face, but his still manner came not from serenity but from a marbled soul. Parmiter was an entomologist—a scholar and lover of insects and all things relating to them. Earth, soil, wind, food, temperature, were responsible for bringing out his sensuality. Today he was driving south to Candor, North Carolina, with three insect sample cases and his lab assistant, Gerald Metbaum. They were coming to collect specimens of a beetle said to make fire.

Parmiter noticed how the woods petered out into the flat landscapes of the Piedmont. This area, the east central portion of the state leading to the coast, was as foreign to him as the sands of Mars. Parmiter knew the area was geologically odd. It had once been very volcanic. Millions of years ago, when Europe and America were connected, it had been underwater. Yet for some reason there were few marine fossils.

The area was unusual for another reason. Grim folklore permeated the culture. Between the sandhills and the coast lay Maco Station where a train conductor, decapitated by a wreck in the nineteenth century, was reported to wander restlessly along the tracks looking for his head, a ghostly lantern marking his presence in the night.

And once a black slave in Arapahoe had saved his master's drowning child and was rewarded with three red rubies. Bandits captured the slave and disemboweled him when they learned he had swallowed the jewels for safekeeping. The natives report that at night the slave appears in smoky blood and horror in the still-standing slave quarters looking for his killers.

Parmiter decided that it was definitely not his kind of country, even though it was only three hours' drive from his college.

As they turned into Candor, Parmiter swerved to avoid a stalled tobacco truck on the road. The two of them were to meet Henry Tacker in Flinger's Grain and Feed Store at one thirty. Emmet, Rose Flinger's son, greeted them amid rows of crates reeking of excremental fertilizer.

"You folks from the college?" Emmet asked.

"Yes," Parmiter said, stripping off his coat, in the suffocating heat. His damp white shirt clung to his torso like wet paper. "May I have a glass of water please?"

Emmet filled a paper cup from a spigot at the side of the building. "We sent them bugs out *two weeks ago*! Took you all long enough to get down here."

"Sorry. It usually does. They went to the Pest Control Bureau and then up to Washington. The Agricultural Research Service. I heard about them yesterday."

"Well, nothing happened! They burned up Henry's peach trees and nobody did nothing."

Parmiter held out the cup for another refill. "No, Mr. Flinger, they did something. They sent me."

Parmiter and Metbaum walked behind Henry Tacker through a

field of short, thick grain under a sun blazing so hot it seemed only inches above their heads.

Tacker said, "Harmon sprayed them last week again, but they didn't even slow down."

Parmiter peered at the dried dusty ground. "I thought you said they were numerous."

"Well, you can always find one if you look hard enough. Harmon found two in his barbecue pit. All the rest are in my peaches."

"What do they eat?"

"Ashes."

"What?"

"Sure! Wood mostly or plants. Ashes."

Metbaum asked, "How come they haven't gotten around the countryside more?"

Tacker said, "I guess it's 'cause they can't fly."

Metbaum pointed out, "In other words, you haven't seen them fly, Mr. Tacker."

Tacker, with an air of long-tested patience, stopped and faced Metbaum. "Sonny, they ain't got no wings. They can't fly. Okay?"

"Okay," said Metbaum.

"Maybe the larvae have wings," Parmiter suggested.

"Maybe. I ain't seen any young'uns though; they all the same size. They ain't much good at crawlin' either."

"Why not?"

"Perfesser, what kind of a bug just sits there and lets you pick it up? It don't run when you step on it and it don't move when you grab it, except for burnin' the shit out of you."

They walked on, Tacker trudging through the heat like Prometheus. Sand poured into Parmiter's shoes and collected in lumps against his blistering feet. At the blackened orchard, they stopped. Tacker surveyed the ground, with hands on hips, and grunted. "There's one there." He nudged a piece of wood.

Parmiter wiped at gnats swirling before his eyes, and bent to examine the two black oval shapes on the wood. He touched one and legs unfolded. The bug stumbled forward, bumped into its companion and lapsed back into inertness.

"Are they all this big, Mr. Tacker?"

"Just about."

Three fast conclusions dropped into Parmiter's mind like tumblers into an oiled lock. The insects' carapaces, or shells, were extremely tough. There were no wing seams along the sides. And they possessed long delicate antennae, almost as long as the body itself and as strong and supple as steel-cored rubber poles.

"I'm going to try something here," Parmiter told them. He picked up the insect between thumb and forefinger, keeping his head back to avoid getting sprayed or stung.

The insect was astonishingly heavy. It nearly slipped from his fingers when he first felt the weight. The legs dangled limply. Only the antennae moved. "Come here, Metbaum."

Hesitantly Metbaum peered over the professor's shoulder.

"What do you see, Metbaum?"

"It has six legs. Three body sections, I *think*. It's an insect, not a spider or . . ." Metbaum looked closer. "Its legs are clawed. Like an aphid maybe . . . something that clings . . . the spiracles are almost underneath it. Look at it breathe!" Metbaum wiped sweat away and observed a faint contraction of the shell at the edge.

"I can feel it breathe," said Parmiter. "Very high metabolic rate, I should say."

"Then how come it doesn't move around?"

Before Parmiter could answer, the insect came alive. The legs splayed and then churned in slow swimming motions. The antennae sweeps became more urgent. "Powerful. Very muscular," Parmiter muttered.

He turned the bug over to examine the belly. The body plates were iron shingles, sealing the underside shut. The legs spoked out like delicate, embracing petals. Jutting prominently from the rear, aimed slightly downward, were two cerci-rear antennae—very stiff and horny, like exhaust pipes. Parmiter touched them. They whirred like wings. A monstrously loud chirping blared, startling Parmiter so badly that he nearly dropped the insect.

Parmiter looked at the cerci. "I'll be damned," he breathed.

"Yeah?" said Henry Tacker.

"You have a six-legged Boy Scout here, I bet. These rear antennae are very chitinous. Unless I'm mistaken, this little fellow starts fires by rubbing them together. It's like starting a campfire with flint."

"Great," said Henry Tacker. "Isn't that just great?"

"Very strange. Cerci are usually just the opposite. They're very sensitive to wind and heat and so forth."

"Yeah, but I ain't never heard of no bug that makes fires. I sure ain't."

"Me neither," Parmiter answered. "The closest thing is the bombardier beetle that scalds its enemies. But that's not this. That beetle can't burn down trees." Parmiter turned the bug around and gazed at its face. "Okay, Metbaum, use your eyes. What's missing from this fellow?"

Metbaum stared. The silence grew. So did the heat. "You got me, Doc."

"Eyes, damn it. It doesn't have any eyes. It's blind as a bat!"

Bainboro College, an extension of the State University, was the hub of a town of the same name, containing some fifteen thousand citizens living in a suburbanite's dream of twisting, quiet, secret, forested streets that stopped and curved back upon themselves much like the minds of the students and professors who inhabited them.

The campus itself, heavily funded by sentimental alumni, was hung with great oak trees through which gravel paths threaded their way, ultimately spilling out onto a flat quadrangle surrounded by class buildings. The school was so garlanded with vegetation that only the clangor of class bells bringing four thousand students out of doors was evidence that anything besides birds lived there.

James Lang Parmiter's office was in Carson Hall where he was rarely visited because of the small terrors lurking in the jars, cages, boxes, and plastic cases on his shelves. All were bugs, all of them brightly colored, many of appalling size—the largest being a South American dragonfly measuring seven inches from wingtip to wingtip.

The fire beetles from Henry Tacker's peach orchard which rustled laboriously through Metbaum's tin can were added to the only other one of Parmiter's specimens that was actually alive and unpreserved amidst the drawers with carcasses pinned to them. It was his prize, an enormous, dull-colored *Gromphadorhina portentosa*, named, whimsically enough, Madilene. Madilene was a female who spent her days in a small wire cage littered with food crumbs, filter paper, and a small water tray. A pair of horns protruded from her head.

She hissed as Parmiter cheerfully entered and said, "You didn't eat your garbage, you idiot!"

Madilene was a hardy, foul-tempered cockroach, one of the largest of its type in the world, measuring four inches in length. She was unquestionably the most aggressive of her species and had been captured by Parmiter in her native Madagascar the previous month.

Parmiter sent Metbaum home and prepared to do a dissection alone. He wrested a bug from the tin can, sat at his office desk with the insect, and gently tapped its legs. The insect's silence worried him. He withdrew a cloth tape and jeweler's loupe from his drawer.

The creature lay quiescently on the blotter as Parmiter measured off three and five-eighths inches from head to tail. The antennae alone were exactly three inches. He examined them through the glass. They were the only delicate part of the anatomy, closely jointed, with a series of small dots—sensory endings—sprinkled along their length.

Parmiter examined the sides of the body for evidence of wings. He was somewhat baffled to find nothing but a smooth, seamless armored case with a plated belly. In the *Coleoptera*, or beetle, the tough front wing sheath protects the fragile rear wings. Period. That definition was what characterized the more than two hundred and ten thousand species of beetle, making it the most common form of life on earth—plant or animal.

Parmiter bit his lip, thought for a moment, and then bent forward even closer, screwing the eyepiece in tightly. He went over the sides of the thorax for evidence of muscle base indicating Paleopterous wings. Paleopterous, or ancient, winged creatures like dragonflies, had wings that were anchored to a narrow base and protruded straight out like aircraft wings, making the insects the graceful gliding dive bombers everybody knew and hated. No wing musculature. Nothing. The fire beetle could have been a Sherman tank.

Parmiter removed the glass and rubbed his eye. He looked at the bugs in the can and the one lying peacefully on the blotter, and as he did so, he forced his mind to flit lightly over the hard black bodies for several seconds to see what his imagination could pick up. Then he closed his eyes and forced the pictures in even tighter. When he opened his eyes again, a slight, cold smile had etched itself onto his face. A couple of preliminary conclusions had formed.

The bugs were sick. Those long powerful legs were designed for running as well as clinging, yet the things just clumsily wallowed through the ash. And Parmiter had a feeling that some kind of sickness had driven them to the surface in the first place. The bugs could not fly—indeed they could barely walk. They could not possibly spread. Parmiter reached both conclusions by a combination of instinct and experience.

In went the eyeglass again and this time Parmiter examined the face. Except for a transverse fissure—the mouth—running across the underside of the body, the face was totally featureless, a blunt, crevassed surface like the side of a black cliff broken only by some horny, flexible tissue at the antennae.

As Parmiter watched, something horrible occurred; the underside of the face split like an opening trap and a glistening, dark pillar of nerve and muscle uncoiled. The tongue curled briefly, like a scooping shovel, then withdrew. The beetle began writhing, antennae reaching trustingly for Parmiter's face. Through his fingers Parmiter felt its labored breathing, the air painfully sucked in through the spiracles.

Parmiter wrote out a detailed description of the fire beetle in his neat, tiny hand emphasizing its lack of features and wings, and its fire-making capabilities. It was now time for a dissection. Parmiter moved into the lab across the hall, carrying the beetle, and set it on the long table surface.

He used a small, silver hammer to crack open the beetle. There was a great amount of tissue. Parmiter put a bit with tweezers onto the microscope slide and pressed it under another piece of glass. While letting it dry a bit he examined the neatly opened body before him.

The beetle had no digestive system. No stomach. No esophagus.

Nothing. Just behind the mouth, Parmiter's steel needle gently traced a strand of beadlike glands, white as pearls, expanding into a fleshy mass in the gut where the stomach should have been. The tissue surrounding these glands was partially eaten away. The visible nerve and blood strands connected with the white substance.

Parmiter cut away a section of gland and put it on a second slide. He did not wait for it to dry but mounted it immediately in the microscope and focused. Parmiter did not even blink. In an ecstasy of panic, he sprang from the bench, grabbed a bell jar covering one of his students cactus seedlings and clapped it over the microscope. He slammed all the windows in the lab shut, closed the door, rushed into his office, and with shaky fingers dialed the number of Fred Ross, the school pathologist. A sleepy voice answered after the fifth ring. "Yeah?"

"Ross? Parmiter!"

"Oh, yeah. What's *bugging* you, heh heh!"

"Get over here now. These beetles are full of bacteria. They're walking germ cultures and I've just cut one open. I put a bell jar over it. Get over here, Ross, *now! now!*"

"Whoa, slow down now. It's two o'clock in the morning and I'm at my worst."

"Now!"

Ross muttered, "Shit." But he came. He wore white pajamas with cupids on them beneath his blue jeans.

Ross peered down at the bug under the jar, yawned, and rubbed his eyes beneath his wire-rimmed glasses. "Well, Parmiter, if any of these pathogens are airborne, this dinky little bell jar is too late. We're both dead." He yawned again and plopped his pot-bellied figure on the bench. "If this really worries you, I'll have to take the microscope, that tin can, and the building into a sterilized lab with me."

"I'll need the microscope back this afternoon."

Ross was rattled. "Okay, look, are you the first one to bust one of these open?"

"Of course!"

"Didn't anybody step on them even down there in that town?

Have any of them died? I mean that place would already be a tomb if the bacteria were dangerous. . . ."

Parmiter's granite expression did not crack a bit, but his body seemed to slump with exhaustion. He sat heavily on the bench. He remembered Tacker telling him about Herman Harris smashing dozens of the bugs weeks ago. "Yes, you're right. I should have realized that."

Ross yanked the bell jar off the beetle carcass, exposing the remains to the air. "Okay then."

"Ross, these things bred underground and I don't think that bacteria has ever penetrated to the surface. I assumed we had no defenses against it." Parmiter made an enormous effort and said the hardest words within him, "Sorry to bother you."

"Hell, that's okay." Once again Ross examined the bacteria through the microscope. Then he withdrew it, wrapped it, and slipped it into his pocket. "I'll set up a couple of culture mediums. Shoot up some rats. Obviously the stuff isn't airborne. You better get some sleep, Parmiter."

"I will. Good night."

"Night."

In the isolation of the lab Parmiter looked down at the blind beetles and wondered if through some mysterious sense they were looking back at him.

September 22

METBAUM carried into the lab a sack containing a salami sandwich, a carton of milk, and his transistor radio with the earplug attached so as not to disturb the general silence of the building.

Parmiter had left a list of instructions on the bench for him. "Remove the antennae from the insects and study their reactions. Try to determine the exact location and construction of their sex organs. Remove a set of cerci and place them on a slide along with a piece of that drumlike tissue from the bug's abdomen."

Metbaum slung his lunch onto the bench and sat down. Parmiter opened the door and glanced in. "I trust my handwriting is legible, Metbaum."

Metbaum answered, "Too legible. I'll be here all afternoon." He noticed the bell jar. "What's that doing here?"

Parmiter described his experiences of the previous night. "Ross is going to send over a preliminary report today. And I also sent some to Raleigh. I don't suppose you'd know Wiley King."

"No."

"He reminds me of you a lot."

Metbaum paused just as he was about to bite the sandwich and rolled his eyes at Parmiter. He lowered the sandwich but kept his mouth open. "That a fact, Doc?"

"Wiley King was one of my students. One of my *best* students."

"Do you ever see him?"

"Certainly not, Metbaum." Parmiter slipped his tweed coat off his gangly frame and loosened his tie. "Never look back, Metbaum. Never."

"Doc, I was always kind of curious. Who did you study with? Anybody I ever heard of?"

"Max Linden."

"That guy at the Smithsonian."

"Yes, I was very young."

"You're not so old now."

"I was old the day I was born, Metbaum. Get to work," Parmiter snapped. He was always irritated when questions got too personal, which, now that Metbaum reflected on it, was whenever he was asked any questions at all.

Metbaum killed one insect with the small hammer and neatly snipped away the small round drum of flesh from its abdomen. He mounted it neatly between two glass slides and taped a label to it. From the cage he withdrew another insect and set it onto the blotter. The beetle clung to his finger before dropping to the felt surface. It crawled slowly to the edge as Metbaum took a small camel's hair brush from his leather kit.

Metbaum hummed in time to the music pulsing through the earpiece of his radio. He stroked the soft brush across the insect's side. The legs ceased wriggling and opened like a fan under Metbaum's caresses. A small horny bump appeared under the abdomen. The insect's carapace expanded and contracted slightly in ecstasy. Metbaum's stroking continued its seductive cadence as he shouted, "Hey, Doc!"

After an inordinately long time, a foul-tempered Parmiter appeared. "What!" he barked and Metbaum remembered that Parmiter did not like people to speak to him.

"I'm sorry. I just thought you'd like to see one of these things having an erection."

Parmiter leaned over his shoulder and grunted. The small bump unhinged from within itself like an egg hatching a complex structure of spidery cranes and machinery.

"That thing must hook onto the female after he's grappled her into position."

Parmiter grunted again.

Metbaum touched the penis. It collapsed swiftly. The insect's legs stiffened outwards again, and Metbaum put the insect back onto the blotter.

"Pick out a female, lock them up and try to catch them copulating."

"Can't."

Parmiter said sharply, "Of course you can, Metbaum!"

"Not from these samples, Doc." Metbaum's wave indicated the line of cages stacked on the lab table. "We've got seven females here, and they're all pregnant."

"*All* of them?"

"Yup. They're carrying egg cases. At least they look like egg cases. How come you didn't notice this last night?"

"I must have been working with a male."

Parmiter straightened up violently as his phone rang.

"What's the matter, Doc?"

"I hate telephones. Cut open an egg case, Metbaum. *Do* something!" Parmiter snapped as he walked to his office.

Ross' lazy voice rumbled through the phone. "Progress report, James. I injected some mice and guinea pigs and an egg with those

35

germs. And I got it all over Petri dishes full of blood agar and jellied nutrients. That pretty much covers anything that could happen. Can I make a suggestion?"

"Yes."

"Send some of these bugs to Raleigh. They have a better pathology lab than I have."

"I've already sent some to Wiley King. Good-bye."

Ross said, "You're welcome!"

"Good-bye!" Parmiter hung up.

Metbaum felt the tiny clawed feet securely, trustingly, grasp his left thumb. The brush's caress had soothed and excited the beetle to a state of trembling delight. Metbaum slipped the scissor blades around the rear cerci and waited till the penis of the beetle dug against his flesh. He snipped. The cerci tumbled into a white plastic cup.

The tiny claws curled into talons of rage. Metbaum felt the shell suddenly contract in shock. The sudden pain diverted the beetle's sexual anticipation into anger, and he clawed and bit at Metbaum's thumb, cerci muscles flexing futilely against his flesh. Had the creature's cerci been active, Metbaum would have been burned clear to the bone, for he felt the abdomen dig tightly against him as a cat grips its enemy in its forepaws' embrace and swings up his haunches to disembowel it. The beetle would not let go.

Metbaum stood and tried to shake the palpitating insect loose. He grasped the body and pulled gently, but the legs held on. Twin needlepoints pierced his thumb. The creature, whose multiple mouth parts were good only for chewing, had nevertheless managed to bite Metbaum. Metbaum cursed and flung the beetle to the floor by banging it against the table edge. As he stomped furiously at the beetle, the bell jar toppled off the table and fell with a crash to the floor.

Parmiter's scowling face looked in. He saw Metbaum, white-faced, with his arms folded tightly, his left hand clutched under his right armpit.

"Try not to smash the place up, will you, Metbaum?"

"Lay off, Doc."

"And none of your smart mouth either. What happened?"

"An accident."

"Kindly elaborate."

"Nothing! I cut off some cerci and the thing jumped and I . . . jumped too. Nothing."

"Those jars are expensive, you know."

"So I'll buy a dozen of them!"

Parmiter bent down and picked up every single shred of broken glass from the floor and placed all the pieces neatly in a pile next to the beetle cage. He did not speak until the floor was so clean he could run his gleaming shoe over it without hearing the grind of splinters. Then he noticed the smeared remains of the beetle on the floor.

"Don't say anything, Doc." Metbaum clutched his hand even tighter.

Parmiter slipped white paper beneath the remains and carried it toward the trash can. "I want you to call Wiley King in Raleigh and tell him to ship some samples over to the pathology lab there. I'll give you his number." Parmiter threw the beetle carcass and paper into the can and wiped his hands before looking back at Metbaum. "All right?"

"I'll call him," Metbaum tightly answered.

Parmiter's gun-turret eyes flicked to Metbaum's thumb, then back to his face. "And wash that cut there. There may still be glass in it."

Parmiter donned his tweed coat in his office. He straightened his tie and shot his cuffs out. He carefully inserted sheets in order into a manila folder. He looked in at Metbaum who was sitting at the lab table and said, "I'm off to class. Listen for the phone please, Metbaum."

Metbaum inhaled deeply and forced a smile at Parmiter. Every day for a solid year Parmiter had asked Metbaum to listen for his phone. The professor was so isolated from people that he had to constantly renew his acquaintance with them, as though they were total strangers. And, besides, Parmiter had what seemed to be a paranoiac fear about telephones.

"I always listen for your phone, Doc. You don't have to ask."

Parmiter stepped into the lab and peered down at the cerci in the plastic cup. "Just chitin, I expect, but still . . ." Chitin was the substance forming everything from the hair of spiders to the shells of lobsters, crabs, and insects. Given the quantity of such creatures on the earth, chitin was the most common life substance, next to chlorophyll, in existence.

"See you tomorrow, Metbaum." Parmiter left.

Metbaum waited until the precise footsteps had gone down the stairs and faded away. Then he went to a glassed-in cabinet and withdrew a bottle of alcohol used for preserving specimens. He poured it freely over his thumb, where the bite formed a little black mound. Then he washed the thumb, dried it, and put on more alcohol. Despite his own specialization in biology, his distrust of doctors was profound, and he did not intend having some cold, silent, mad doctors shooting some strange chemical into his veins with excessively long needles.

A secretary told him King had left for the day but had assigned students to pinpoint the insects' diet. "I doubt if he'll learn anything for a couple days, Mr. Metbaum."

"Tell him to get some pathologists onto them, would you?"

He wrapped a bandage tightly around the thumb. He looked at the beetles and shuddered. Metbaum had never felt the cold grip of entomophobia—the fear of insects. A strong fear of heights had once inspired him to study phobias; in particular, why huge insects which—with their multiple antennae, faceted eyes, and mouth segments—were nightmares of horror to most people and no more bothersome than a plumbing diagram to him.

He had learned that when the human mind cannot resolve painful conflicts—conflicts so severe they could impair functioning—some part of the imagination wraps up all the parts of a problem into the shape of an insect. Or a sharp-pointed object. Or a rat. Or a snake. Or a drastic fear of heights or enclosed spaces. The vindictive, possessive, destructive mother becomes the terrible shape of the black widow which tenderly embraces at the moment she stings. It is far easier to loathe and kill a small, nearsighted, shy, clumsy, and vulnerable spider than to kill one's actual mother.

When he discovered this, Metbaum determined never to tamper

with his acrophobia; indeed he would encourage it. It protected him from something far worse in his past. Without psychoanalysis he would never know what it was and he was not particularly interested in opening any Pandora's boxes in his head anyway.

Metbaum knew the loathing of the beetles was not a true phobia. Harmless as insect bites usually were, they were unpleasant even to one as sanguine as he. The alcohol burned and then cooled the wound beneath the bandage. That was reassuring for some reason. Metbaum put out the lights and went home.

Nothing further happened with the insects until Wiley King called two days later.

September 24

KING had spent the previous two days collating results on the diet tests his best graduate students had devised. He had taken the lined charts, listing the chemicals disgorged in wads from the insects' mouths, and matched them with breakdowns of their droppings. Since he could not believe his eyes, King had taken the notes home and read them while drinking a bottle of bourbon and looking at the sun rising through his living room window.

Then he called Bainboro College and was told Parmiter would not be in until eleven. The girl put him in touch with Metbaum who had been doing dissections since seven in the morning. King said, "Ask Parmiter to call me back."

"Telephones give him very heavy traumas, Doc. I'll give him a message if you want."

"Still hates telephones!" King chuckled. "Well, are you ready for this, Metbaum?"

"I'm pretty stable."

"This insect of yours eats carbon."

"Carbon what?"

"Carbon and nothing. *Pure* carbon!"

After a moment Metbaum said, "That needs help sinking in. You want to lay it on me again?"

"Bacteria inside the insect feed off one another's toxins and produce different toxins which are absorbed again."

"That's not possible," Metbaum replied. "It's like perpetual motion. I mean if all the bacteria eat is carbon, I mean, if only one of the pathogens absorbs just carbon, it would level off to the others eventually. It can't go upward. . . ."

"It's happening, Metbaum."

"It's still not possible." Metbaum heard Parmiter's door open and shut. He was early today. "You can't build life chemicals with just one element. . . ."

"I know all the arguments, boy! I tell you that's what it does!"

Metbaum thought about calling Parmiter and getting him to listen in on the phone, then decided there was no use in King getting scalded so early in the day. "I guess we better concentrate on pathology. Identify the bacteria; try to figure out the chain of digestion."

King asked, "Is it contagious?"

"No. In fact, we cannot culture it in anything so far."

"Neither can we." King lowered the shade further, turning the white morning September light into a yellow shaded square. "Mr. Metbaum, two of our females have hatched young. Are all of your samples pregnant?"

"Yes."

"Have you managed to make any of them copulate?"

"No. They may be inhibited by captivity though. A couple females here gave birth, so maybe they're ready."

"Do you think they can spread?"

Metbaum said firmly, "I don't see how."

"Nevertheless I'm contacting the health commissioner. I wouldn't care for another fire ant fiasco even if it were justified." Millions of dollars had been spent in the South trying to wipe out a tenacious little ant that built enormous piles of earth in pastures. Farmers claimed that cattle would nudge the mounds and lick the ants that poured forth in droves and eventually die from the still-living creatures chewing away in their stomachs. Entomologists claimed that the creatures were harmless. The farmers won. Planes dive-bombed pastures with spray. Men filed through fields with poison guns. After a year the fire ant's Armageddon became mankind's humiliation. The creature not only survived the massive attacks but thrived on them, building bigger mounds, enraging more apoplectic farmers, and eliciting reams of syrupy metaphysical prose about life's tenacity from scores of biologists. One of the most vocal of these was Parmiter who annoyed his classes by reminding them that humans could never breed or adjust as well as the vermin that crowded in on them all their lives.

"Anything else?" asked Metbaum.

"Yes. I'm going to have that farmer's chasm concreted over. The state will pay for it if we recommend it. Tell Parmiter to contact Max Linden at the Smithsonian, too."

When Metbaum entered Parmiter's office, the professor slid some papers quickly into a drawer and folded his hands on the tabletop. "Well?" he snapped, obviously not glad to see him.

Metbaum told him King's discoveries. Parmiter did not seem surprised. His sharp-planed small head snapped up and down to keep Metbaum moving with his descriptions. "Very good. Wiley is good at this."

"I can't believe it!"

"All life is carbon-based, Metbaum. Carbon is a world in itself, a universe, in fact. You could spend your whole life in organic chemistry, Metbaum, and its totality will still not completely unfold. It's only logical we would find something living that could become infinite."

Metbaum was not quite sure what he meant, but he could tell by Parmiter's tightly clasped hands that he was not up to expounding.

"He also said you should call Max Linden."

"I shall. Anything else?"

"He wonders why they won't copulate. Me, too."

"Ever hear of the eruption of Mont Pelée in Martinique?"

Here he goes again. "That's an island, right?"

"In 1902 Pelée wiped out the city of Saint-Pierre. Two days before, the surrounding jungles became saturated with newly hatched snakes and insects. One plantation was attacked, literally, by centipedes. Nature equipped these creatures for the catastrophe weeks ahead by getting them all pregnant and insuring births. The same thing happens in deserts just before siroccos."

"Before *what?*"

"Windstorms! I've seen it myself. Bedouins predict serious storms by the amount of vermin crawling about. They breed in the millions. Nobody knows how they sense climate changes, but they do." Parmiter turned to his briefcase to signify the end of the meeting.

Metbaum lingered. "How come these things don't copulate?"

Parmiter's face took on a basilisk gaze. His voice was honed to an edge with annoyance. "Because they're already pregnant! And they became pregnant because their climb to the surface was at least as traumatic an event as volcanoes or storms are to other insects!"

Slip one last one in and then bolt. "Why did they come to the surface. . . ."

"*Food!* Get to work, Metbaum!"

Parmiter very carefully slid open his desk drawer and withdrew the papers he had hidden when Metbaum had entered. For some feverish moments he jotted down in a curiously crabbed, faint scrawl his own shorthand onto a yellow pad. The scrawls covered most of the page and comprised—comprehensible only to him—every bit of information Metbaum had related from Wiley King. The notes took only five minutes.

Beneath other sheets listing the characteristics they had so far learned about the beetles, he stapled the new sheet. The top page was blank but for two lines:

Order: *Coleoptera.*
Suggested Formal Designation—*Hephaestus parmitera.*

Hephaestus was the Greek god of metalworking and fire, that culture's version of the Roman Vulcan. Parmiter inclined toward Hephaestus because Vulcan served Jupiter, while Parmiter's beetles, like Hephaestus, were servants of no one. Whether the name was Greek or Latin would not, he was sure, be questioned by Linden. "Hephaestus" designated the fire they made. "Parmitera" stood for himself.

Parmiter harbored a growing feeling that they were his. Like his own loneliness, the beetles inhabited caverns buried quietly and darkly away from the real world, the difference being that their caverns were underground caves, while his caverns were the carefully erected walls he had intricately built in his life against people. He had made his small frame house as a hideaway. One day the beetles might share it with him, and he might inherit their strength by watching them. But that was later. He must be secretive now. Dignified. Conceal things. Plan. Watch himself. *He must not be laughed at!*

Metbaum did not look up when Parmiter, carrying his briefcase, stuck his head in the door and said, "By the way, Hallowell tells me you did a fine paper the other day."

Metbaum felt a thrill. Grades were not to be announced until next week and Hallowell's physics course was a choking mouthful to him. "Oh, come on, Doc," he said.

"He went out of his way to tell me." Parmiter's slick face bounced back the sun flooding the lab. Parmiter had an extremely good smile, with small, strong, white teeth. It surprised people and made them change their minds about his personality.

Metbaum set down the tweezers and rubbed his eyes, tired from peering through the microscope. "I guess I'll be in school another semester."

Parmiter grinned happily. Hesitated. Then finally said, "Yes."

"Thanks for telling me, Doc."

"Yes." Smiling.

"So you're off to class."

"Yes, off to class." Now the smile was nailed onto Parmiter's face like a painting but was still attractive. "Well, keep it up, Metbaum." Uncertainly, hoping he had cheered Metbaum up, Parmiter walked away, down Carson Hall into the morning sun.

"Righto," muttered Metbaum, separating a leg from a dead beetle with tweezers.

In the ashes of a cage he noticed that a female had hatched her young. The infants were tiny periods, almost invisible among the grains of burned leaves.

METBAUM heard Parmiter's pen scratching in his office as he walked softly down the hall to the lab. He was late and did not feel like explaining why. He set his books on the lab bench and looked down at the insects. And within thirty seconds he had run to Parmiter's office, smashing the door open and startling the professor, who glared speechlessly at him. "Doc, have you seen them this morning?"

Parmiter shook his head.

"You better get over there."

Metbaum pointed out the beetles that had hatched the day before and the original samples. Parmiter would not have been able to tell them apart otherwise.

"These are the ones that hatched yesterday. They have tripled their size inside twenty-four hours, Doc. By tomorrow they'll be full-grown adults." Metbaum picked one up. "This is physical growth, not any dippy Mayfly life cycle; these damn things are *growing!*"

"So maybe they'll die off that much faster, Metbaum." Parmiter did not seem particularly impressed. The life-spans of insects varied enormously, from eight to twelve hours for the adult Mayfly to years for the cockroach. And rapid growth did not seem any more amazing to him than metamorphosis in which the insects like dragonflies or butterflies became three different creatures before maturing, a fact comparable to humans being born as fish, spending their adolescence as gorillas, and winding up as *Homo sapiens*. "I expect it's a mutation the bacteria gave them. Early maturity would be a sure survival gift when you consider what conditions underground must be like. And carbon is so basic a life substance the creature must metabolize it into use almost immediately."

Metbaum looked at the huge infants. "There's something wrong with these too. Look at them. They can't move any faster than their parents; they're sick too."

Parmiter examined them carefully, nostrils flaring slightly. "Everything is food to them."

"I should grow so fast. I still don't understand where they get food from."

"They just do the same thing bloodsuckers do, Metbaum, only on a grander scale. You study ticks or bedbugs, you find organs inside them that produce vitamin B, similar to those bead glands that are infested with bacteria. Vitamin B is the only thing blood doesn't have as a food, and it's a necessary substance."

"It's hardly a case of producing vitamin B. The bacteria does everything."

"Yes. Metbaum, this beetle evolved exclusively underground, and I wouldn't be surprised if they were older than anything walking the earth today. They were friends of the dinosaur."

"Why would they go underground?"

"They were trapped by volcanic activity. The sandhills were very volcanic once. They were trapped in caverns where the only food was lichen or moss or fungus or whatever, and with the bacteria's help they thrived on it. Between twenty-five and fifty million years I should say."

"In that case why did they come out!"

"Like I said! Food!"

"You said they thrived. . . ."

"Metbaum, kindly use that appendage on top of your body! They migrated because conditions had become intolerable. Overpopulation maybe, fungus disease that destroyed the moss maybe."

"You sure, Doc?"

Parmiter looked at Metbaum, face surprised. "There is no other possible explanation."

"Why haven't they come out before?"

Parmiter sat on the bench and looked at one of the insects with its legs tucked under it. "Do you know anything about the San Francisco earthquake, Metbaum?"

"The San Andreas Fault. The fault runs down . . . the fire . . ." Metbaum blinked rapidly. "The fire. You're joking!"

"Well, look at them! They look like rocks with their legs tucked in. Who would notice them after an earthquake anyhow; who notices bugs? Well, one thing is certain. We must breed them."

45

"Why? Every female here is carrying an egg case. We'll never run out of samples."

"Sick samples. We don't know what's wrong with them. We need healthy specimens."

"I don't know. They're producing pheromones. . . ."

Parmiter looked up. "How do you know that?"

"You can smell them." The sweetish smell emanating from some of the cages, particularly the night Metbaum had cut off the cerci of the beetle, was unmistakable. Pheromones were sex attractants, a substance secreted by certain insects through glands lining their sides. It appeared when the creature was aroused.

"Doc, don't you think we ought to just see if they can be poisoned?"

He had struck some nerve in Parmiter. The silence was cold before the entomologist spoke. "Why?"

"Just in case . . . you know. . . ."

"What are they going to do except burn a couple of peach trees? They'll be dead in a month."

"Doc, you sure they cannot spread?"

Parmiter's glance broke away. "I don't see how." Then he changed the subject. "Come in here a minute, Metbaum, and bring a male with you."

In his office Parmiter crumpled a sheet of hamburger wrapping into a glass ashtray and dropped the beetle on top. Then he struck a match and set the paper afire. The paper curled in flame around the beetle. Its legs curled tightly and it shuddered once. The paper became ash, and blue smoke filled the office. The legs uncurled, lifted the bulky body up, and turned it around. Then the beetle began eating ash.

Parmiter said, "Well, I just wanted to see."

"Like I said, Doc. I really don't think you want to breed these things. You know?"

Each spent the afternoon dissecting a beetle and preparing slides. Metbaum carefully wrote up his notes and gave them to Parmiter who noticed the swelling bandage on his thumb. "What's that?"

Metbaum guiltily clasped his hands behind his back. "She put the bandage on too tight."

"She?" Parmiter blinked.

"You wouldn't know her, Doc. I got all the females in two cages and the males in one and it's kind of crowded so. . . ."

"Use Madilene's. Put her in that shoebox over there. I'll get a cage in the morning."

Metbaum slipped a heavy glove on and reached for the huge roach. She hissed so loudly, Parmiter barked, "And be gentle with her, Metbaum."

In using Madilene's cage for the fire beetles, Metbaum made a simple mistake that would have had him expelled from any lab in the country. He forgot to change the filter paper lining the bottom of Madilene's cage. He sprinkled in a heavy layer of ash, thoroughly covering the paper, and dropped in four male fire beetles. Then he relocked the cage. On his way out he leaned into Parmiter's office and said, "See you tomorrow, Doc."

Parmiter, in the middle of his dissection, did not even look up. Metbaum shrugged, slung his leather bag over his shoulder, and walked out of Carson Hall, flexing his tingling thumb.

Parmiter listened carefully to make sure the lab was empty of everybody except cleaning women. He combined Metbaum's and his notes on the beetle's nervous system onto typed sheets and inserted them into a manila envelope with an address on it. MAX LINDEN. THE SMITHSONIAN. Then he locked the envelope inside his desk drawer and pocketed the key.

His hand on the light switch had just shrouded the floor in darkness when he heard it—a ghostly whirring chirp that rose infinitesimally in the building. Parmiter listened, not moving. The fire beetles were chirping.

Parmiter tiptoed across the hall and stood at the dark entrance to the lab. His hand inched slowly up. Then suddenly the lab was flooded with light.

The four beetles in Madilene's cage were clinging to the sides. Beneath them the filter paper, several sections of which had been cleared of ash, was clean and white. Unburned. Untouched.

The chirping of the beetles grew louder, more insistent. One dropped to the floor of the cage and paced it, bumping into corners and feeling with its antennae. On one of the exposed spots, the beetle stopped. His chirping became constant and loud enough to reverberate down the hall. Parmiter listened carefully. The chirp did not have the raw, throaty sounds of hunger or food burning. It emerged as a single unbroken trill. It was, in fact, a song.

The difference between Parmiter and his colleagues lay in the speed with which Parmiter discarded wrong answers, like food or temperature variations, and translated the subtleties of insect motivation into something resembling human emotion. The beetles were not hungry; they were unhappy.

With a dark, unerring, empathetic certainty Parmiter looked directly at Madilene's shoebox. The beetles were running around on her filter paper. They were responding to her sex pheromones. Parmiter could tell by the desperation of the chirps and the movements of the bugs. The meaning was frighteningly clear. The beetles were not beetles. They belonged to the order *Dictyoptera*. Cockroaches.

Parmiter curled his lip, slapped his clipboard down on the lab table, and crossed the hall back into his own office where, after a moment's riffling through his drumfile, he found Metbaum's home number. He plugged the phone into the wall and dialed the number.

"Metbaum!" he bellowed at the groggy voice. "You used Madilene's filter paper for the bugs."

After a pause, Metbaum said, "Yeah. Guess I did. Sorry."

"Why didn't you tell me?"

"I said I was sorry! Did you call me at this hour just to. . . ."

"Goddammit, Metbaum, these aren't beetles at all! They're roaches! Cockroaches!"

"Now how do you know that, Doc!"

"I *know!* Metbaum, listen. I need more samples of these things, more than are hatching, more than I've got. You've got to go to Candor first thing in the morning and get some. Lots of them, Metbaum, understand?"

"What I'd really like to understand is how you know they're roaches."

"One was reacting to Madilene's pheromones."

"How do you know he wasn't reacting to something else?"

Sudden rage made Parmiter's voice brittle. "Metbaum, don't question me. Understand?"

Metbaum quietly answered, "Doc, if you say they're rhinoceroses, I'll go along with you."

Parmiter wiped his face. "Good, good. Sorry I shouted, Metbaum. You mustn't question my judgment though. Never do that. It's not necessary, Metbaum."

"Sorry, Doc."

"Trust me, Metbaum."

Again a pause, then, "You got it, Doc."

Parmiter pulled the phone jack out again. He transferred the males out of Madilene's cage back into their crowded one and replaced them with females. When they were separated from their source of agitation, the insects' cries faded away. Presently Parmiter smiled at the silence. He liked it; it was soothing and peaceful. Good, old, cheerful silence.

Jordy Harris felt the hairs on the back of his neck rise and stiffen as he smelled the wood smoke wafting through the empty, cavernous warehouse into his office. He was working late tonight, straightening out the forms in his ledger, which had been incorrectly filled out by a new girl. Jordy stepped quietly out of his office onto the warehouse floor and stood perfectly still. Except for a few twigs and dust the floor was clear of tobacco. The burning smell was stronger, mixed with the leftover odor of tobacco. The smell came from nowhere, yet everywhere.

Outside, at the loading ramp, he heard a car whiz by, radio bellowing through the night. Jordy grabbed the two fire extinguishers on the floor and walked to the loading dock, his feet making booming clacks in the warehouse. He sniffed the air.

Adjacent to the ramp, a sagging wooden door, secured by a rusty bolt latch, led to a storage space beneath the warehouse. Jordy yanked the door open. Blue smoke blasted out in clouds, choking him. Jordy reached inside and switched on the light which gleamed through the clouds of smoke rising from three barrels in which rakes, hoes, and junk were piled.

Jordy looked down at the floor. A large black insect scuttled painfully across the threshold. Jordy cursed in disgust and slammed his boot down on the bug. He felt its hardness beneath his boot, a hardness that did not give under his full weight. When he lifted his boot, the bug paused an instant and marched on. Jordy stomped again. And again. And a fourth time before he crushed it.

The smoke roiled against the wooden crossbeams from which the naked bulb was suspended. Jordy sprayed the barrels with the extinguisher, splattering foam across the floor and burying the sputtering flames under thicker clouds of smoke. Jordy coughed and moved the door back and forth to clear the smoke out. Then he waited, heart pounding in his chest.

A movement in the corner dragged his eyes toward a rusted grass seeder. Three black insects. Jordy sprang at them as they tried to scuttle beneath another barrel. By jumping repeatedly up and down, Jordy managed to kill two of them immediately. As he jumped, the third unleashed a series of chirps that were quite the loudest he had ever heard from a bug. The bug desperately stumbled toward the door, veering behind a stack of pipes as Jordy kicked the stack apart, exposing the insect on the naked floor and sending it on another slow run for safety.

Again Jordy headed it off. Then jumping to block each lunge, he backed the bug into a corner next to a water pipe. The insect's chirps rose to a despairing shriek before being silenced by the force of Jordy's boot. Jordy felt warmth through the sole of his boot as the insect's struggles subsided. He looked at the underside of the boot and saw that it was burned nearly to the insole.

He called his wife to tell her he would not be home for dinner. Then, in spite of the fact that it was nearly midnight, he called the Agriculture Department in Raleigh, then Pest Control. No answer.

He woke up Henry Tacker. "Henry, who's that feller from the college who come down here for your ticks?"

"What for?"

"I caught a couple of them in here. Come on now. . . ."

Tacker muttered, "Parsley. Pitty . . . pum . . . permy . . . Shit! Party . . . somethin' . . . *I* don't know, Jordy . . . *Parmiter!* Yeah."

"Spell it!"

"Go fuck yourself, Jordy . . . Hold it—I woke Ruth up." Henry muttered to his wife, "It's Jordy—naw, shut up and go back to sleep," then said to Jordy, "Yeah. Parmiter. Dumb name, if you ask me."

"An' he's at Bainboro?"

"Yeah, that's where he is."

Jordy tried Bainboro and got a night watchman who hung up on him. Information listed a James Parmiter on Forest Avenue. Jordy tried the number. A thin, girl's voice said, "I'm sorry, but the number you have dialed is out of order. Please try. . . ." Jordy hung up.

He searched with a flashlight the ground around the warehouse, peering at the folds and ridges of sandy earth for the telltale black knobs. He found nothing. He spent the night on a cot in his warehouse and, instead of sleeping, listened.

September 26

PARMITER looked with distaste out over the ranks of faces in the classroom. Although his briefcase was on the podium before him, he did not use notes. He clasped his hands behind him and cleared his throat. He looked neat, cool, and self-contained as usual.

"Ladies and gentlemen, the lecture today is not part of Bio 4, so you need not take notes. Some of you may be acquainted with a species of insect, discovered in the southern part of this state a few weeks ago. It was erroneously classed as a *Coleoptera*. Last night I discovered it was a cockroach. Thus, it seems to me to be a good chance, indeed it may be the only chance you will have, to learn some facts about this creature. The cockroach is *persona non grata* all over the world. It is not exotic enough to be a subject of serious lab study; it is not glamorous or eccentric enough even to photograph. In spite of the fact that you will share your life with it wherever you go, you will not ever take it seriously, so this is about the only chance you'll have."

Even from the back, Metbaum could feel Parmiter's power spread like a wind across the students. These were the times when Metbaum truly admired the entomologist. Parmiter despised teaching, but nevertheless it brought out the best in him. He never knew how eloquent he could be.

"I don't know how many of you are religious, but if you are—as I confess I am—then you must necessarily observe the lushness, the sheer staggering abundance of life on this blue planet as the surest example of God's attention. God loves life, the preachers tell us; nature cares for our children, the naturalists tell us. This is all very reassuring until you look at it. For you will discover that the lush living things on this earth are, overwhelmingly, vermin. If God made life, then by the sheer variety of his invention, he found bacteria, insects, reptiles, and vermin far more interesting than man.

"And God made them well, better in too many respects than he made the primates. The cockroach will survive atomic war as will bacteria and other insects. Man will not. Man has been on the earth in his present form only for fifty to a hundred thousand years at most. The cockroach has been around *without change* in design for some two hundred and fifty million to three hundred million years. When you think of God's glory by the life He has created, you had better well be ready to include the fangs or eight eyes of a spider or the pervasive cockroach before you sing any hymns.

"If you look up the cockroach in reference books, you will find several interesting facts. It is very closely related to the fish and its nearest insect relatives include praying mantises, grasshoppers, and termites. The roach is so perfect in basic design that evolution is unnecessary. It flourished during the carboniferous period, the age of jungles and great forests. Essentially cockroaches are tropical creatures, lovers of warm climates and damp lands.

"Cockroaches lay eggs and care for their young. Some give birth twice to the same infants, which is to say that they carry them in an egg case in their vulva after they've been hatched. They do not go through pupal, larval, or any metamorphosis stage. Cockroaches can survive without heads. Some can even learn in this lamentable condition, although they eventually starve to death. They lay eggs in packets called ootheca—egg case to you. For different species, egg gestation is three to eight months, although this particular species breeds several times faster. Their diets cover nearly everything. Paste. Wallpaper. Ink. Shoe polish. Their own dead. Bedbugs. They love beer, and certain shipboard species are fond of finger- and toenails. They eat anything man eats, cooked or not, *anything,* which is why they love us so much.

"You are doubtlessly under the illusion that cockroaches are filthy. Basically they are not. When they aren't copulating or eating, they are cleaning themselves. And although they carry pathogens for a variety of diseases, such as polio, they *rarely transfer them.* There isn't an entomologist alive who has not eaten them on field trips. I myself was served three different species inside of a very excellent enchilada I had in Mexico. I finished the meal. I'm still here.

"Although they crowd together in groups of thousands in small places, they are not really a social insect. They can shrink to three-quarters of their size, sometimes half, when running; this is why they are difficult to catch around crevices. They leave a smell behind caused by chemicals called quinones. These are definitely unpleasant, for quinones ruin the taste of food. But they won't poison you.

"Cockroaches, particularly the Madeira roach, are being studied in one area of cancer research. When the nerves supplying certain glands in this creature are severed, tumors form in those glands. Tumors appear also when hormonal balance is upset in certain species, especially when endocrine glands are tampered with."

Parmiter stopped pacing and glanced at his watch. "That, in ten minutes, is what I know about cockroaches at the moment. Oh, just one last thing. There are more than thirty-five hundred species alive today. One went to the moon with the first astronauts, I recall reading. You may go."

Parmiter was the first one out of the classroom.

Metbaum spotted the professor on the campus grove after the building had been emptied of students. Parmiter was squatting on his knees on the campus grass, just beneath an oak tree.

"Doc?"

Parmiter held a hand up for silence. "I don't wish to do this in public, Metbaum. I assume no one is around."

"Nope." Metbaum looked around at the campus walks which were temporarily empty. "You lose something?"

"No, I'm gaining something. Watch, Metbaum."

In the big oak a bird chirped from the green dappled branches. Metbaum then realized Parmiter was locking eyes with a squirrel that squatted motionlessly some five feet in front of the professor. The squirrel's black button eyes blinked at Parmiter, trying to make him out. Parmiter's back stiffened, then his neck muscles, then his arms, and from the back of his throat came soft, crooning sounds. With a quick, perky hop the squirrel sprang for Parmiter's welcoming fingers and laid its neck up for throat rubbing.

Metbaum cracked a twig. The squirrel rocketed up into the oak branches and vanished. Parmiter stood up, wiping grass and twigs from his immaculately pressed suit. He adjusted his tie, shot his cuffs, and smiled happily. "Just a parlor trick, I wanted to see if I could still do it."

Metbaum gazed up into the tree and saw only leaves. "I think you did it, whatever it was."

Parmiter picked up his briefcase and dusted it. He began walking rapidly toward Carson Hall, with Metbaum following. "Metbaum, there are symbols more basic than human speech. Mannerisms would be a better description. Birds take off from a branch en masse from some silent invisible signal. Have you ever seen that?"

"Is it important, Doc?"

"Then you haven't noticed it!"

"Doc, I stopped noticing it back when I caught lightning bugs in New Jersey."

"And the way bees sense that the queen is ready for flight. What makes an entire species communicate instantaneously, Metbaum?"

"I don't know, Doc."

Parmiter's eyes had a flinty, faraway look as though the concrete walk that he stared down at was not enough of a challenge. "Man used to have that gift, Metbaum. He could talk to the earth and all the creatures on it."

"Cockroaches, too, eh?"

Parmiter frowned at the student, his mind already on another subject. "Metbaum, I believe you've lost weight."

Besides being alarmingly thin, Metbaum's face was sallow, with eyes sunken. A fresh bandage was around his thumb. "I don't get it, Doc. You're the second one to say that today. I feel great!"

Parmiter had paused on the walk, eyes searching his young assistant's face to the young assistant's acute embarrassment. Parmiter said, "Take care of yourself, Metbaum. Nobody else will."

"I'm fine. Really."

"Good then. What did you think about the pseudo-lecture this morning?"

Metbaum carefully chose his words. "I'm afraid I find cockroaches pretty disgusting, and, good as it was, your lecture didn't change my mind."

"I have a feeling, Metbaum, that *Hephaestus parmitera* will gain your respect, if not your love, within the next few days. We're going to be working hard on it."

That was the first time Metbaum felt the touch of fear that would soon turn into an avalanche of terror. Parmiter, whatever he knew, had chosen his words well. Metbaum's trust had been secured by curiosity.

In Henry Tacker's field, Metbaum put the seventh roach into his can, then looked up at the wiry irrigation sprinkler, ejecting a hemisphere of constant spray through which rainbows glinted.

He said to Henry Tacker, "What's that for? I've been seeing them all over here."

Henry grunted and spat. "Them bugs. I'm keepin' everything wet."

"Well, you won't need to."

"I wish you'd tell Jordy that. He liked to had his warehouse burned up last night, Mr. Mertbump."

Metbaum felt the leaden headache settle more heavily on him, producing irritation at Tacker's taciturnity. "They cannot migrate. You must not worry about them." Metbaum stood, and swayed.

Tacker steadied him. "Now hold on there . . . easy . . . easy. . . ."

Metbaum flung his arms free. "I'm perfectly all right."

"You don't look it, feller, you look like you're ready to shit cactus."

In spite of his nausea, Metbaum laughed.

Tacker clapped his back, "Come on up to the ole house for a nip and let's us call Jordy. He's awful worried."

"I know. I'm sorry, Mr. Tacker. Here." Metbaum scrawled out "Wiley King" and his number on a piece of paper. "Call King first because it'll take me two hours to drive back to school. If you can't get him, wait till six tonight and have Mr. Harris call me at home at this number."

Tacker scratched the back of his neck and looked doubtfully at the paper. "Yep. Okay. I'll tell him. Sure you don't want to come in for a while?"

"I have to get back." Metbaum started off across Tacker's lumpy field to his car on the road. "You really won't need sprinklers."

"I just think I'll keep 'em goin' for a while, Mr. Metblomb. Take care now!"

Wiley King dipped his thin little brush into an even thinner layer of clear, sweetish-smelling fluid. Holding a male *parmitera* firmly in two fingers, he painted the substance on the insect's sides. The fluid was as precious as gold and King had access to it only by luck. It was called seducin, and it was the male pheromone of the *Nauphoeta cinerea*. Gathered only in minuscule amounts by slaughtering hundreds of that species of roach, the substance produced violent sexual reactions in females of the same species. Since the female *Nauphoeta* responded to a variety of species, King hoped female *parmiteras* would do likewise.

King dropped the male *parmitera* on the table. A dozen females instantly swarmed around him, antennae flickering, mouths gobbling at his shell. The passion reached the point where King feared the male was endangered. As he brushed the females aside, several females tasted the aphrodisiac on his fingers and attempted a run up his sleeve.

The phone in his corner buzzed. King found himself talking to Jordy Harris in Candor. "Hello?"

"Yeah, hello? I'm Jordy Harris down in Candor, and we sent

some bugs over there a few weeks ago that burned up Henry Tacker's peaches and last night a couple of 'em liked to burn my warehouse down. . . ."

King chewed a fingernail. "You checked all the tobacco, Mr. Harris?"

"We been doin' that! We been checkin' everything—leaf, drivers—and Pest Control said we was to let them know if we see any, an' that's just what I'm doin' now."

"Well, did Mr. . . ."

"Lemme finish now, mister, lemme finish now. Listen here. I don't know how these things got into my warehouse. And if all our lookin' for 'em for this month was a waste of time, if they got past us—an' skinned if I know how *that's* possible—then they could be over half this country see 'cause we ship *everywhere*! I don't know how they coulda done it, but *they got into this warehouse!*"

King felt the cold tentacle of fear. He sat down at the desk. "Did Mr. Tacker unload at your warehouse?"

"No, sir. Henry grows peaches not tobacco. Now I think we got to do somethin'. I can call Sam Tucker down here and get the truck logs and find out where they been goin' all week. . . ."

"Now hold it, Mr. Harris, hold it for a moment. . . ."

"But dammit, the Pest Control place told us to call. . . ."

"Wait a minute, though, wait! How far could they have gone?"

"Well, there's over forty shippers in Montgomery County, and with peaches or cotton you just go till you get a good price."

"Do you know any others, Mr. Harris, who've seen the bugs?"

"Uh . . . no."

"How about fires then?"

"Uh . . . no. 'Cept Jimmie Holdbam burned his truck up from smokin'. What kind of poison should I use anyhow?"

"Poison doesn't work. Spread ashes around your place, Mr. Harris. If they have a lot of food, they won't burn anything." King started on a second fingernail. "I cannot understand how they traveled. It's not possible especially if Tacker doesn't. . . ."

"I guess I can run over and ask him if he's seen them. . . ."

King's breath caught. "Run," he said.

"Yeah, he's just up the road."

King's fear popped like a bubble, leaving him empty except for irritation. "Now damn it, Mr. Harris, how far exactly is Tacker from your warehouse?"

Jordy was slightly subdued by the anger on the phone. " 'Bout four miles, I guess. Five." Then he saw the implication and exhaled. "I know what you're thinkin'."

King's relief made him feel happy. "When I said they couldn't travel, I didn't mean to imply they couldn't walk. But these insects are sick, Mr. Harris. They cannot breed or fly. They'll die off in a couple of months."

As usual Jordy was impressed by education. "You're sure now? They can't do nothin'?"

"I'd advise you to watch out for accidents like what nearly happened to your warehouse."

Harris was soothed by King's well-modulated voice. "Okay. You know what you're talkin' about, I guess. Thanks, Doc."

At noon King got into his car and drove to a pizza stand for lunch. On the way he passed a group of police cars surrounding a stalled Chevrolet on the street. The car belonged to one of his students who stood disconsolately by the curb. King invited him for a ride.

"Just gave up on me. The mother just died."

King nodded. "Where you going?"

"Home."

"What happened?"

"I don't know, it just coughed all the way up from Montgomery County."

King looked at him. "Didn't know you were a farmboy, John."

After the stalled car was chained to the tow truck one of the cops straightened up, wiping his hands. He paused when his partner suddenly said, "Freeze, Billy."

"Why?"

His partner walked up to him with drawn club. He flicked it at the cop's pants cuff. A fire beetle flipped onto the street. The cop smashed it with three whacks of his club. "It was going up your pants leg. You can relax now."

As a medieval picture of murky hell, the jungled grounds of the storage and refinery plants straddling the Jersey turnpike would have done quite nicely. Lighting came from the flares of fire billowing from towering stacks. It fitfully illuminated the pipe mazes, domed storage tanks, cracking plants, railroad tank cars, and the faint dust-shivering vibration on every fitting, caused by the grunt and hump of invisible machines pumping chemicals at high speed.

It was eleven o'clock. The industrial flats slept under the smog of sulfur and petroleum fumes. The door to a guardhouse, huddled beneath the mountain of a storage tank, opened and a fat man named Talbot stepped out to unbutton his coat and smoke a cigarette. Talbot looked at the dipping, sliding spears of headlights from the turnpike traffic. A truck loaded with produce had stalled out there this afternoon, causing a three-car pileup. Talbot inhaled smoke and exhaled. He scratched the wad of fat under his chin and loosened his tie.

There came a soft, musical, lively sound to his ears, which rose over the clank of the steel-clad machinery in a fenced-off pipe section. Crickets, he thought. They reminded Talbot of being young and having a backyard in which to sit and drink tea in summer as dusk fell. Talbot shouted in the door, "Hey, Mickey, come on out and get this!"

A second guard joined Talbot and cocked his head, listening. "Valve friction?" he asked.

"Naw! Crickets, asshole!"

"How'd they get in here?"

The chirping rose. Others in the darkness began singing.

"They're all over the place."

"Yeah," Talbot said happily, "pretty."

Both listened.

The huge storage dome behind them split like a blossoming

flower revealing seething fire in its bowels that split the night apart. Five million gallons of flaming gasoline washed over the guardhouse and its occupants.

Like hell triumphant, the volcano of fire surged high into the sky, a maelstrom of torn, rumbling debris churning about its base. The shock wave roared across the ground on a flat trajectory—ripping apart spurting pipes which boiled into liquid flame, crumpling lacy steel girders, overturning the railroad tank cars and telescoping them together like cardboard tubes—and slammed head on into the turnpike traffic like a sledgehammer of air, skidding the cars to the highway's edge in a ballet of squealing brakes and smoking tires.

The thunderclap hurricaned through the refinery grounds tumbling running men head over heels into wire fences and pipe junctions in a blizzarding tangle of earth, steel, and pipe fragments. The shock wave crossed the highway and tore up the atmosphere across Jersey and finally expired with a window-rattling *whump* in lower Manhattan. Bells, lights, horns, and particularly sirens of every description heightened the pandemonium of explosions.

In the seven-minute interval before the fire-fighting equipment arrived, five people died and a dozen were badly burned. The firemen noticed in the five-mile-square caldron small groups of insects crawling through the grass, weeds, and puddles of oily water dotting the grounds. The firemen did not think them important enough to remember. Which was why the television crews and reporters who descended on the scene also did not think them worth mentioning in the news.

September 27

THE girl clutched her books tightly to her breast, as though they were teddy bears. She peered out at Parmiter through twin barriers of falling straight hair that continually threatened her vision. Her eyes widened in fear at the sight of Parmiter's shelves. "Uh . . ." she began.

"They're all dead, young lady," said Parmiter.

"Wow."

"You say Metbaum sent you?"

"Um. He's going to be late, he said. He can't get his car started."

"Oh, thank you very much." Parmiter turned back to his desk, then, realizing she still stood there, turned back to her. "Anything else?"

"Yeah, I'm thinking. What's that brown thing there?"

Parmiter looked at a plastic slab in whose transparent depths was encased an enormous insect, nearly the size of a human hand. "Goliath beetle. Biggest in the world. Want a look?"

"I'm looking. Oh! Gerry wanted to know if you were going to call that man in Washington."

"Max Linden? I'll get around to it."

"Well, see you." She waved, without dropping her books. Parmiter saw her go. So Metbaum had a girlfriend. Parmiter felt a pang. For some reason he hoped he looked presentable.

Max Linden as usual was preoccupied. In the silence of his office at the Smithsonian, he opened a package from Bainboro College and out tumbled a sheaf of papers and three dead fire beetles.

Just before sitting down, Max Linden unhooked the heavy silver watch and chain and unbuttoned his waistcoat. Linden always dressed with the weight of his title. Head Taxonomist, Division of Insect Identification, Agricultural Research Service in the United States Department of Agriculture. Linden had never been to the Department of Agriculture. His life centered in the banks of filing cabinets containing the labeled bodies of thousands of insects. He also had a staff of fourteen specialists.

Linden immediately recognized the fire beetles. And he recognized the dry, neat handwriting as belonging to that dry, brilliant student of his from years back who had always sat at the back of the classroom trying to disappear into the woodwork. Long time ago. Linden wondered what he looked like now. He had looked forty even then.

Order: *Coleoptera*.
Suggested Formal Designation: *Hephaestus parmitera*.

Linden picked up the copy of the Baltimore *Sun* lying on his desk. Three photos on the front cover depicted a four-block five-alarm fire that had ravaged Baltimore the previous afternoon and was smoldering even now. Linden could tell nothing from the text or photos. The city was unsure of the fire's cause.

The North Carolina State Bureau had sent four samples of this insect to his attention, along with descriptions of its inflammatory activities. He had once talked by phone to Wiley King. He was ready for anything. When he read the description of the insect, he concentrated on the description of its nervous system and weaponry. He wanted to know about those aspects.

The *parmiteras* had heavily muscled legs within their steely shells which would have classed them as runners except for the size of the nerve trunks serving them—not to mention the fact that they just did not run. The nerves triggered the muscle reactions and the speed of these reactions depended on the distance across the nerve synapses, empty junctions between nerve fibers across which an impulse must jump like a spark leaping across terminals. Cockroaches had tremendously thick leg nerves with short synapses; they could travel at full acceleration only five-hundredths of a second after light hit them. Loss of thickness in nerve trunks, a more complicated delicate system, slowed down physical reactions. The insects, as their complexity grew, gained somewhat in information-retention abilities—often mistaken for intelligence. The beetle was a paradox—muscles plus numerous nerves.

Linden turned a page. A title read WEAPONRY.

Parmiter discarded the obvious ones—biting mandibles, venom sacs (although the saliva, as King had said, was very acidic and tickled the skin) and no quinones. That was notable, for it was the most subtle of insect artillery. Quinones were repellent chemicals of enormous complexity, often with a horrific smell that wrecked the muscular coordination of enemies. Stinkbugs and certain cockroaches left this nerve gas behind and often it lingered for days. Metbaum had carefully searched for signs of quinone-producing equipment like glands, muscle or nerve clumps, anal passages with contracting ligaments or fluid bladders. Ninety percent of the search was useless, as Linden ruefully knew, for Metbaum would only have had to smell them to see if the beetle used quinones. His searching hands and dissection razor would have told him within hours.

Nerve masses lay at the bases of both antennae. And a small, fleshy drum between the cerci, with a nerve connection running to the brain, measured heat, telling the insect whether dinner was cooked enough. With no eyes, the drum and the antennae were all that could penetrate that fireproof shell and let it know what was happening in the world.

For some moments, Linden read over that part of the report. Then he called his secretary. "Do you still have yesterday's *Times*?" She brought it in. On page one was an article about a group of fires in the south Bronx. This report appeared with the blaring photos and headlines about the Jersey refinery disaster. FIVE PEOPLE KILLED BY EXPLOSIONS AND SMOKE DAMAGE. The concussions had been felt as far away as Connecticut. Thirteen million dollars. The news had been clogged with it ever since last night. Cause undetermined.

Linden spread out several more newspapers that he had been keeping for three days. Resting his chin in his hands, he followed a pattern of fires he was not sure really existed. A tobacco warehouse in Lynchburg, Virginia. Blocks in Richmond and in Baltimore. Linden turned pages and let random incidents hit his eye.

A car had exploded and burned on the Jersey turnpike the morning before the Elizabeth refinery went up. The Lincoln Tunnel had been closed down for three hours. A car had caught fire. And in the south Bronx, fires broke out at the Hunt's Point produce market which received shipments of fruit and produce from all over the East. Tomatoes. Lettuce. And peaches from the South. Trucks and flatbed cars brought them in every day.

Of course it had been an unusually hot summer, tinder-dry in ghetto housing. Fires were not unexpected. And, even if the bugs could travel, surely such fat black monsters would be noticed. Wouldn't they? Of course, tenements such as those in Baltimore and the south Bronx were full of bugs and rats besides. Cities lived closer to insects than the countryside did. And who would notice during a fire? They wouldn't. Or would they?

Linden dialed his secretary. "Get Sheldon at Agriculture. And after that, call what's-his-name at the Museum of Natural History in New York. He's in the biology department."

Everybody was on vacation. Linden called James Parmiter. No answer—the phone was out of order. Then he called Wiley King in Raleigh. He found himself talking to a girl. "Oh, sir, he's out for the day. He's gone down to Candor to get some roach samples."

"Anything interesting?"

The girl said "Ohhh," as if a puzzle had just been explained. "Those fire beetles, sir, are really roaches. Doctor Parmiter in Bainboro found out last night."

"Roaches! Good of him to let me know; I've got his samples here. He named them after himself. Has King been keeping track of them?"

"Well, sir, now he has, ever since we got Mr. Harris' phone call."

"Who? What?"

The girl told Linden about Harris' rage. Fire in the warehouse. Linden felt a cold breath run the length of his spine. "You mean they can travel."

"Well, sir, we don't know how that's possible, and besides Mr. Harris lives just across from Mr. Tacker. . . ." She went on like that until Linden interrupted her, extracting a promise from her for a call from King.

He said to his secretary, "Ready for a bit of telephone combat?"

"I'm ready for anything."

"Get Pest Control. Ask them to connect me with the city administration in New York. What we've got to do is get hold of the New York fire department or the mayor's office and tell them about *Hephaestus parmitera*, I mean tell somebody who will react. There's just a faint possibility that some of these insects got up there, and they'd better be told to keep an eye out. Use the Smithsonian's name for weight. And try not to panic anybody. Not till we're sure. Okay?"

She spent the bulk of the morning fighting a city bureaucracy by long distance. First came the Bureau of Fire Investigation, day service. "Good morning, I'm calling for Doctor Max Linden of the Smithsonian in Washington. . . ."

"Washington Heights, lady?"

"No. D.C. Will you please connect me with. . . ."

"D.C. You calling from Washington, D.C.? This is New York City, lady!"

"I know that. We have possible information on the fires. . . ."

"Which fire, lady?"

"Among others, the Hunt's Point. . . ."

"Oh, that was a short in the fuse box. . . ."

Next she tried the Borough Headquarters Communication Division which said someone would call back, but no one did.

The Executive Offices on Church Street sent her to the Fire Prevention Complaints Division then to the Fire Prevention Information Center which bounced her back to the Executive Offices again, where somebody angrily took the call. She buzzed Linden. "Sir, I have a Mr. Brody on the line."

"Who is he?"

"He's an assistant something, sir. For God's sake, take the call!"

Brody listened for thirty seconds to Linden before crackling the phone line. "Bugs! Cockroaches! If this is a crank call, I'll lock your ass up, mister!"

Thirty more seconds of Brody's rage blew both their tempers out of control. When the secretary looked in, she saw Linden, face purple, half standing behind his desk, shouting, then, abruptly, looking at a silent phone.

"I have never been treated like that in my life!" he bellowed, then calmed down by cracking pencils in half with his right hand. "They have to log the calls. And it's just as well until we're sure there's something there. Get Parmiter. Send pigeons if you have to."

Jordy Harris' bulk loomed over the frail, pale figure of Wiley King. King squinted up at the mountainous man who barely obscured the fierce sun.

Jordy was furious. "What you fellers got in your damn heads I could put in my blue tick's asshole, I swear. You're supposed to know these things!"

King tried to look in control of the situation, but his surroundings—the hot field, the glum, sullen farmers, and Harris' unconcealed contempt—were so primitive that he could fake nothing, particularly not the sinking fear and humiliation that faced him.

They were surrounding a stalled tractor with the plow raised. A farmer had felt it go dead in the middle of a furrow and called a mechanic to come out and repair it.

King asked meekly, "Any more in there?"

Harris bent under the tractor, a length of pipe in his hand.

The exhaust plumbing slithered and wound the length of the vehicle, disappearing in the engine block.

Jordy hit the pipe against the exhaust. From within it came a muffled chirp, lengthened by echoing metal. Jordy clanged away two, three, four times. The chirping moved slowly toward the exhaust opening until a *parmitera* squeezed through the dust-clotted entrance and dropped to the sand where Jordy crushed it.

"Goddamn farthead intellectuals!" Jordy barked at King. "They was never in no fruit or tobacco. They was *inside* the cars! You shoulda known that, dammit! They probably crawling all over Russia by now! Fartheads!" In disgust Jordy threw the pipe into the sand.

The most humiliating part, King reflected as he drove back, was that he had even told the answer to everybody, had read it in his own reports. Carbon monoxide.

The most ready source of carbon on earth was the American highway. The roaches would have crawled into every car, truck, and tractor in the county. They would have bred and, silently, unnoticeably, infiltrated other vehicles. An automobile was a feast for them. Oil. Gasoline. They would never have stopped hatching, and concealed in autos, they would never have been seen. They would have smelled carbon in the air, for the atmosphere was choking with it. They did not have to move. Superhighways carried them everywhere, far past Montgomery County. Always hatching, always changing cars, spreading farther and farther. . . .

In Raleigh, King called Max Linden. The conversation was brief. Linden said, "I shall inform Agriculture and get the government behind this. Keep in touch. And try to call Parmiter about it."

Metbaum walked into Parmiter's office that evening, looking even paler than he had been during the day. "That was King, Doc."

Parmiter looked up from the microscope. "Biting the bullet again, is he?"

"No. The *parmiteras* are all over the country." Metbaum described the roaches in the exhaust systems.

Had Parmiter slapped his forehead, gnashed his teeth, or chewed up the scenery in frustration, Metbaum would have felt reassured. Instead the entomologist's stony features became more and more still, more quiet, more frigid until it seemed as if he would crack into thousands of indestructible splinters at the slightest touch. Metbaum stepped closer to him and saw that Parmiter's eyes did not follow him; instead they remained looking at the wall where Metbaum had stood. Finally Parmiter sat down. His hands lay in his lap, his head was slightly bowed. "Thank you, Metbaum."

"What now, Doc?"

"We have to . . . I don't know, Metbaum. I think we should sleep first of all. How could we be so. . . ."

"Yeah, I know the feeling, Doc."

As though the light bothered him, Parmiter shaded his eyes. His fingers made small clasping movements. "I don't know, Metbaum. I sometimes wonder what good we are. This is inexcusable."

"I hope not, Doc. What I don't get is why we haven't heard anything about them. If they're doing any damage, I mean we'd know by now, right?"

"Maybe, maybe not. That's not what bothers me."

"What does?"

Parmiter gripped his hands together tightly and rested his chin on them. "I was wrong. That's what bothers me."

"Oh." And because Parmiter said nothing more, Metbaum left.

Metbaum picked up a paper on his way home and searched it for some hint of *Hephaestus parmitera*. There were enough fires all right. Baltimore. Lynchburg. But there were always fires. At the bottom of a paragraph though, Metbaum found a sentence. Just a hint. In New York, a columnist noted that the mayor had missed four press conferences in a row. The columnist had asked a member of the mayor's staff why, and the staff man replied only that it had been a long hot summer. Very hot.

September 28

LIKE all cataclysmic events, the Hephaestus Plague was perceived by millions of people only in bits and by a very few in its awesome breadth. These few included the city administration of New York which, within the space of a few days, had mapped out in the mayor's home at Gracie Mansion, with small colored pins, the most devastating wave of fires that had ever hit the city. Even to the press, the extent of damage was not known as a single picture. Hunt's Point had been destroyed. Blocks of Harlem had been flattened by fire storms. The Upper West Side crawled with fire engines and raged with sirens. It was summer after all. A very hot summer.

That morning the police commissioner sat in the mayor's house and looked out over the barges plying the morning mist of the East River. The mayor silently read several papers which the fire commissioner had given him that morning. They detailed the results of twelve hours of the most massive series of raids ever undertaken by the police of any city. The raids had been conducted with search warrants and clubs and were aimed at the home of every suspected arsonist, black revolutionary, brown revolutionary, mafioso, pimp, gun runner, and arms supplier in all the five boroughs from Queens to Staten Island. The raids had been conducted in as much secrecy as possible, and as such the twelve hours of their occurrence had quietly transformed New York into a police state.

The police looked for arms storage and evidence of conspiracy. The mayor conferred with the heads of all the great cities that had suffered fires and all had agreed: The tenacity, ferocity, and increasing destructiveness of the fires were meticulously planned by an organization bigger, better supplied, and more efficient than any yet known.

The fire commissioner summed it up. "The fires all begin on the ground floor. They begin half an hour after each other, so that instead of finding a house, a ladder company is likely to find a block burning when it arrives. Arson is definitely not ruled out."

The police had leaned on their stoolie systems. Informers met in dark bars with officers. Old phone numbers were called and reminded of past favors. Cuban and Haitian exile groups found polite, crew-cut men attending their monthly gatherings, and capos heard the telltale hollow bong of a telephone tap.

The mayors of the Eastern cities, along with their police staffs, were the only ones who knew the full extent of the fire storms that had arisen in the late summer balminess. And as with all great fashions, New York City would be the first to present the results of civil insurrection to the rest of the country.

All that was necessary was to keep the extent of the fires out of the newspapers. This they succeeded in doing. It was why neither Parmiter, Metbaum, Harris, Linden, nor any of the entomologists in the country familiar with *Hephaestus parmitera* had felt worried until recently.

The mayor lowered the last sheet of paper and looked at the police commissioner. "I see," he said.

"I'd call it conclusive, I would. You just cannot hide that many fire bombs and stuff. Not for two weeks anyhow, sir. It's just not possible."

"Well, how are they doing it?"

"It's got to be an out of state outfit, and they have to be in deep hiding. I don't know though—we've been leaning so hard. The crazies are under surveillance and TPF has been traveling with fire marshals since last week. They have to have friends somewhere." The police commissioner looked tired.

"What about that dynamite factory on Houston Street?"

"They just had dynamite. No gasoline. No Molotov cocktails. These political types go in for bombs anyhow. The raids were a waste of time frankly."

The fire commissioner cleared his throat. "For that matter, we couldn't find much traces of gasoline anyhow. I'd like to know what they're using." The fire commissioner stood up. "If I'm not downtown in twenty minutes, it'll be noticed."

They watched him go. Three minutes later he was back again. "The phone," he said. "Some guy's been calling from the Smithsonian since yesterday. Some guy named Linden; he's with the Department of Agriculture."

The call was connected through a speaker system so that all of them could participate without actually holding a phone.

Linden's dry, faraway voice peeped out of the speaker for three uninterrupted minutes. He described the bugs and the futility of poisons. The mayor looked at the fire commissioner who gazed at the phone as if it were one of the bugs just described. The mayor said, "Insects, John?"

The fire commissioner's mouth opened and closed. "You're asking me?"

"No reports like that?"

"God, no! Who looks at bugs in this city anyhow."

"Is it possible?"

"The way he described it . . . Let me do some quick checking."

When the fire commissioner returned after twenty minutes, he sat heavily in a chair. "That guy's right. I talked to five fire marshals. After I mentioned it, it seems all of them remember seeing bugs. *After* I mentioned it. *After!*" The fire commissioner sneered in disgust. "We'll be getting confirmation in a few minutes."

The mayor turned back to the phone. "That man you mentioned who knows these things. I'd like to fly him up here."

"You mean Parmiter? That's not possible."

"Why not!"

"Well, he pulled all his phones out of the wall for one thing. And forgive me, he's a bit crazy for another. He'd never do it."

The mayor looked incredulously at the commissioners. One of them suppressed a laugh.

Linden continued, "I wish I could come up with something that would kill them quickly, but I'm afraid you've got nothing but trouble ahead of you. Maybe winter will slow them down, especially if it's wet, but . . . well, for now we're all stuck with them."

Outside, an East River barge slowly surged past the mayor's

window. He looked out at it and thought for a second that its afterhouse, misted by the morning fog on the river, looked like a tombstone. "That's not encouraging. But I thank you for being honest anyway. What are your suggestions then?"

"Long-range mostly. I believe that the only possible weapon is natural enemies. We just have to find the right one. A bird. A spider. A lizard. Maybe even dogs or cats. Some kind of predator. Also another type of predator may be good at killing the eggs, some kind of parasitic wasp. But it all involves lab work."

"How long will that take?"

"At least till spring. With lots of experimenting. And assuming the bacteria isn't cultured."

The mayor looked at his watch. "We shall have to clear every vehicle entering the city."

The fire commissioner said, "I believe, sir, we shall have to halt traffic completely. Close off the major streets at scheduled times except for emergency vehicles and public transportation."

The police commissioner said, "And restrict incinerators. And smoke effluents from stacks . . ."

". . . oil burners . . ."

". . . Con Edison . . ."

". . . harbor traffic . . ."

The list grew longer under the mayor's secretary's scribbling. When they had finished, she read off all of what they had said. For some reason it still seemed funny to the sanitation commissioner, who had been silent till now. He had been in politics too long. He was the one to break the silence. "Lots of luck," he remarked, looking out the window at the East River. They could hear the fire sirens in the distance.

September 29

METBAUM gathered together tape cassettes of the roaches' chirping pattern and placed them neatly on the lab bench. He had been late arriving at the school. It had taken an hour to have his car checked at the service station for insects in the exhaust plumbing. Parmiter was late, which was unusual for him. Metbaum tested a couple of cassettes.

Wiley King had sent over a chart showing the results of tests of the insects run off by the Pest Control Bureau. Using an audio spectrometer, King measured the exact pulse rate and duration of different songs. King had locked two roaches away from ashes for two days until they began chirping out of hunger; indeed the chart said they had begun to melt the thin metal walls of the cage. Hunger chirps came in pulses at a rate of two hundred a minute. The mating call of the *parmiteras* was continuous but at a higher frequency.

King had placed roaches in refrigerators and used candle flames to see if the same hunger and mating songs changed frequency at different temperatures. They did not.

When he had lined up the cassettes, Metbaum looked out the window to the campus square below. A station wagon with the call letters of a TV station had been parked there for half an hour. Waiting for Parmiter. Metbaum impatiently glanced at his watch. The lab door opened suddenly.

Parmiter sat down at the bench. His face was white and his hands shook.

"What's the matter, Doc?"

"Eh? Those . . . people, Metbaum! I'm being followed! They were waiting outside my house. Look at that—they're even down on the campus."

Metbaum looked at the station wagon. "They're just reporters, Doc."

"I don't want to talk to them, Metbaum."

Metbaum looked at Parmiter's face in awe. The entomologist was terrified. The hard, sharp face had gone soft with fear, leaving him weak. Parmiter mopped his forehead, then looked fearfully toward the hall. "I managed to get classes canceled up here. Told them it was an emergency." He looked as though he expected something horrible to come through the door.

Metbaum nearly lost his temper. "This is an emergency, Doc! People are scared!"

"I don't want to talk to those people, Metbaum!"

"You have to!"

"I don't want to!" Parmiter's voice cracked a bit. Something like panic lurked behind the eyes. "What do they want with me? I'm doing all I can; I'm trying to breed them; I'm trying to find a poison! You talk to them, Metbaum, you do it!"

"They're not going to bite you, Doc!"

"You do it, Metbaum!" Parmiter's eyes were almost pleading. "You handle all that, will you?"

"I'll have to plug the phone back in."

"Then you answer it."

The second Metbaum plugged the jack in, the phone began ringing. It was the New York *Times*.

The calls did not stop. Parmiter was busy, Metbaum explained. He gave a biography of Parmiter to each caller. No, Parmiter would not be available for interviews. Yes, they were in touch with everybody. After two hours of this, Metbaum had still not been able to get back in the lab. He pulled the phone plug out himself and looked in on Parmiter.

Parmiter sat tensely on the bench, hands clasped tightly between his legs, eyes looking frantically around the lab. He had not done a thing all morning. The cassettes were untouched. He jumped in terror when Metbaum opened the door. "God, I thought you were one of them, Metbaum!"

"I'll get rid of those guys downstairs, Doc."

"Thank you, Metbaum." Parmiter agitatedly fingered a cassette. He went back to staring around the lab. Or daydreaming? Metbaum wondered. What a character. Parmiter was frightened by people. Metbaum had once heard a hint about Parmiter's past. A death had changed him or something like that. Something sad.

Several reporters had climbed the stairs into the building, and Metbaum met them in the hall in a flurry of flashbulbs.

"Who are you?"

"Uh . . . Gerald Metbaum. Look, can we go downstairs. . . ."

"Parmiter here?" several asked.

was knocked clean onto its back. Bruno bit. He clawed. Fang and leg slid off the roach's obsidian shell. Bruno used up his venom after three useless bites.

The emotionless ferocity of the fight chilled Linden. The leg-scrabbling, blind, ripping attacks had no dignity to them. The spider and the roach embraced in a tangle of legs and toppled head over feet around the box. Then Linden quite clearly saw how the *parmitera*'s six legs gripped the exhausted spider tightly and pulled the furry body toward its abdomen, where the cerci waited. A raucous chirping boomed up from the cage.

Bruno went mad with agony, trying to tear loose from the roach's gripping legs and drilling cerci. The legs became a blur of desperation. A faint wisp of smoke rose. The spider's movements became jerks and ceased. Linden opened the cage and rather sadly withdrew the spider's burned limp form.

One of the staff members said, "Why don't we try a bird then? Since we're starting at the top, it ought to be something big. Falcon or . . ."

"Parrot," snapped Linden.

Inside a standing gold-wired cage, the green and red bird flapped its wings once, then snatched up the roach in its beak, and shook the roach back and forth trying to crack its shell.

Then, standing on one leg, the parrot gripped the bug with the other leg and tore with its hooked beak at the roach, pulling off two legs just before the insect curled them up beneath its body. The parrot flung the bug against the cage bars. It picked up the bug and violently shook it, trying to bite through the shell.

The *parmitera* managed to get a tight grip around the beak. It chirped once. Instantly, in a whirlwind of feathers, the parrot dashed the insect to the floor and flapped up to its perch with a piercing squawk. Linden and the others waited. The parrot did not attack the roach. In fact, it avoided the roach.

When Linden checked his watch, he realized the fight had taken forty minutes. He looked at the parrot fluffing its feathers. The roach poked around in the papers of the cage.

One of the staff said, "Give him a day and he'll make gravy out of that bug."

Linden replied, "It's the burning. Psychological, as well as real. The damn thing's just caved in from shock." He looked at the parrot in disgust. "One hour per insect and it didn't even slow it down. That won't do at all."

October 1

BY that morning more than seventy universities across the country had received samples of the *parmiteras*. In many of those states, field stations maintained by pest control bureaus had amassed large numbers of the insects already and were trying to poison them.

A spectacular fire that burned for seven hours in Baltimore brought threats, speeches, and disclaimers from government people in the Department of Agriculture, which, in turn, increased the journalistic heat on everybody working on the insects.

Parmiter's press evasions took on a paranoid tinge. He now did not even wish to be seen by anybody. He was out of the house at five in the morning by the back door, went down his neighbors' lawns and through back streets to Carson Hall. He always arrived soaked from the sprinkler systems through which he had run.

That morning, as he crossed the quadrangle, he was horrified to see three reporters who saw him at the same time. They chased him into Carson Hall, and he barely managed to get the door locked and hide in Hallowell's office, quaking in terror for three hours before he finally caught his breath.

Metbaum was trapped by the reporters when he arrived at the school for an eight forty-five class.

"It's Baltimore now, as well as New York City. What are you people doing about them bugs?"

"We're working on them."

"What the hell's the matter with that Parmiter?"

"He's very . . . shy."

"Shy! He's crackers!"

Metbaum flared. "I know what the roaches are doing. I don't need to be told. Every school and pest control center in the country is trying to stop them. Now you people quit picking on Parmiter. I'll let you know if there's any progress!"

Parmiter was calm when Metbaum, in a foul temper, came upstairs to the lab.

All but two of the female roaches had hatched their young. The lab and hall was a deafening racket of chirps. Every jar, box, and cage was filled with over a dozen times as many roaches as they had contained two days before.

Parmiter and Metbaum had to shout over the insects' shrieks to make themselves heard. "The hatching rate is speeding up," cried Metbaum.

"What did Linden say to you?"

"No dice. They've got to find something to penetrate the shell. Even a parrot couldn't do it. He said a praying mantis put up a pretty good fight."

"He still thinks natural enemies are the answer. He's wrong, Metbaum!"

"I don't see why that's a bad idea! He's going to New York tomorrow. They're doing research on dragonfly larvae at the Museum of Natural History. They can punch through anything."

"So we'll turn the country into a nice shallow country pond, eh, Metbaum? Breed some larvae, some snails, a few lily pads? Or maybe supermaggots and drop in the beetles? I repeat, they're wasting their time! Bah!" Parmiter glanced at the legions of screaming insects. "They cannot copulate. Something is preventing it. The answer lies *there*, Metbaum. And we've got to find it before they overcome it themselves. All it takes is one successful mating somewhere in the country, just one, and we'll never be able to stop them." Parmiter carefully inserted a hairlike tungsten wire into a battery case. "Get me two of the adults, Metbaum."

"Want me to open it?"

"No. We're about to try something rather difficult. There may be some malfunction in the brain that prevents pregnancy. The only way we can find out is to map the brain."

While Metbaum held the struggling insect still, Parmiter gently drove a needle into its head, just enough to penetrate the shell without damaging the brain. He inserted the thin wire into the opening. The *parmitera* went limp.

"Dead," Metbaum muttered.

"Keep trying. I didn't even get to turn on the electricity."

They killed four before one of the insects stayed alive long enough for Parmiter to turn on the juice. He, flipped a switch on the battery, and the roach's thunderous chirping brought an answering racket from the others.

"Ah, that's his sex call. Metbaum, remove the brain and see what part the needle hit. Carefully now, Metbaum."

By evening they had pinpointed the locus of the hunger and sex drives and the muscular centers of the *parmiteras*. Metbaum drew a diagram marking out the points where damage caused antennae movement and continuous chirping. The brain resembled that of a cricket; this was not surprising since roaches and crickets are closely related. Two mushroom-shaped bodies, *corpora pedunculata,* located at the front were major centers for nervous function. The singing emanated from them.

All the glands, including the endocrine glands, were undamaged. Tissue walls, only a cell thick, were clear and supple. Nerves were perfect.

At eight that night Metbaum and Parmiter looked at each other in mute exhaustion. They did not see any need to elaborate to each other. There was absolutely nothing wrong with either the roach's brains or any or its organs—no reason whatever why they should not be mating.

"Do not pass go. Do not collect two hundred dollars," said Metbaum.

"Shut up, I'm thinking!" Parmiter barked.

In Raleigh, Wiley King lowered his clipboard to the lab table and looked at the *parmitera* lying still and mute in the Petri dish. He looked at his two assistants. With an effort he resisted the growing flood of exultation within him. And by their strained faces King could tell they were fighting their feelings too.

Mold coated the bottom of the dish. Green, furry balls of it coated the insect's feet.

Two days before, on a hunch, King had smeared blood agar tainted with the penicillin mold onto a piece of burned wood and fed it to a roach. Yesterday, the insect had not moved in the dish. It did not even respond to prods from King. Today, they could detect breathing only with difficulty. The creature's legs were limp and splayed, the heavy body resting on them like a rock on a spray of twigs. It was paralyzed.

"Get out two more and try plain bread mold. Billy, call the Health Department and tell them to send over all the antibiotics in the morning."

"What if they don't eat it?"

"Inject them. Rub it into their shells close to leg joints and spiracles. If it works we'll worry how to spread it later. But we'll have to see *how* it works."

The students looked down at the insect.

King continued, "It's worth a damn big try. Kill the bacteria, not the host. It may be something like an antibiotic spray. Or a powder."

By evening, the insect still had not moved. The mold covered the legs and part of the shell. The cerci did not respond to probes; the mouth would not open even when pried.

An assistant said, "We should call Linden, Ross, and Parmiter. I think it'll have to be more powerful than penicillin. . . ."

King interrupted. "Just call Linden for the time being. Let's not spread it around till we're absolutely sure."

October 2

AT LaGuardia Airport, Max Linden was met by four men from the Museum of Natural History. There was little traffic on the expressway into New York because of restrictions on gasoline-burning vehicles. Linden saw the spires of Manhattan through a low, hanging smoke haze that swallowed up the tops of the buildings.

A scientist said, "They stop traffic at midday except for the fire engines. The bugs hit Harlem and the South Bronx hardest—all the poorer areas, in fact. That's where the buildings are in bad shape."

Thousands of people walking—that was the most incredible sight of all. Their shoes made a clattering thunder on the sidewalks. Sirens pierced the air, which was dim enough to justify turning on neon lights even though it was only three thirty in the afternoon.

Linden saw some of the streets lined with broken glass and trash. The scientist said, "It's just thousands of small fires actually, trash, alleys, parks. When they banned traffic, it gave the fire engines more room to move around so they get around better than ever. It could be a lot worse."

The car pulled up to the soaring steps leading to the Museum of Natural History. Linden looked down Central Park West at the overcast and the blinking neon. On dim gray days like this, New York was profoundly depressing. Linden said, "Looks like the dead of winter. That's what this town was in when I first came up here. Well, gentlemen, let's make damned certain things *don't* get any worse!"

In a recently setup lab Linden saw tanks filled with scum and the developing larvae of damselflies and *Trichogramma* parasitic wasps. The shelves were packed with cages full of scorpions, centipedes, snakes, and every description of lizard, from iguanas to slit-eyed geckos.

Linden shook hands with a wizened, blinking man with a hoarse voice named Reynolds. Reynolds pointed down to a small tray containing an open *parmitera* egg case. "We're being very scatter-shot trying to get a line on types of predators that affect them. Once we do, we'll narrow it down to a particular species which we can scatter around easily. This egg case now. We tried to get a Trichogramma to lay eggs inside it. She couldn't penetrate the outer shell so we opened the case ourselves to see if they even bothered then."

"And?"

The scientist spread his hands. "It didn't work, but at least the roach eggs were killed. We're trying fly maggots now. I don't know. We're also still trying to culture the bacteria."

Linden followed the scientist from room to room, all crammed with cases of *parmiteras* and machinery. The smell of a biology lab—that strange, musty, pungent odor of life—assaulted him even in the dean's office.

Reynolds was a zoologist. He talked nonstop for one hour. "The young begin growing six hours after birth. The bacteria count decreases in the blood and increases in the digestive tract. Look here."

Linden looked into a microscope at a fetus of a *parmitera,* no bigger than a dust mote.

"The infants have complete digestive systems and a low bacteria count. The stuff is transferred to the young through the saliva, and then it supplants all the digestive organs. The bead glands form them."

"Saliva!"

"That's right. The female carries the egg case around in her mouth and washes it continuously until just before hatching. But, you see, the thing is they do not inherit these pathogens at conception. The infection has to be introduced from outside, even to the young."

Linden said slowly, "They were infected several million years ago during the volcanic ages. The infection became benign after generations and helped the insects adjust when they were trapped under the earth. The carapace is hard, sealed, in order to keep oxygen out, except from the spiracles, and keep the pathogens in."

Reynolds nodded. "I guess so."

"So in order to culture the germs, Reynolds, we have to duplicate conditions as they were then! The earth's atmosphere has changed; its temperature has risen."

Reynolds wordlessly led Linden to a vacuum tank. "We tried. We thought we had a colony going in an atmosphere heavy with nitrogen and ozone. They all died."

"We cannot breed them, so we cannot poison them during gestation. We cannot poison them during adulthood. It's got to be a natural enemy, Reynolds. That's all there is left to us."

The king snake writhed. The jaw disarticulated, then the reptile's mouth snapped over the hard shell of the roach. The roach chirped. The legs clawed at the snake's face. Enraged, the snake thrashed and

82

tossed the insect against the wooden floor, jaws clamped tightly, trying to crush it.

Linden and the others watched in silence.

The *parmitera* wrapped its rear legs around the underside of the snake's jaw and struggled to free itself of the mouth. The roach chirped loudly. The burn changed the snake's mute rage to pain. It whipped and opened its mouth, flinging the roach away.

Linden bent down and picked up the *parmitera*. He examined the shell. Nicks. Dents. Scratches. Other than that, no damage.

"Keep trying," said Linden, dropping the insect back into the case.

They drove him to an uptown hotel in late afternoon, past clanging fire trucks. Reynolds said, "One other thing, not that it makes any difference. The fire department found out that new fires start within an average of half an hour after each other.

"In the same neighborhood?"

"Sometimes in the same building where they were just extinguished. For some reason the bugs start burning away all at once as soon as the fire trucks arrive—well, here we are."

Linden was numb. As he stepped out, he saw a *parmitera* trudge through a tangle of trash on the sidewalk and drop into the gutter. He crushed it with effort. "Don't get too used to them, Reynolds. What the hell . . . !"

In the lobby of the hotel were heaps and piles of bedding, mattresses, brightly colored clothes, and furniture, as though people were moving in. He heard transistor radios and shouts from children. Puerto Rican and black families milled around on the marbled floors.

Reynolds said, as though apologizing, "It's a housing crisis. So many slums have been burned that something like a half million people are being housed in these places. Emergency housing was used up the other day, so I guess it was just a matter of time before the class places were taken over."

Linden looked down at the poignant heaps of lamps, framed pictures, and clothing. He heard the shouts of Spanish voices, saw the suffering look of the uniformed doormen and porters. A handball hit him in the side of the head and he looked down into the scared face of a black urchin with his hands crammed in his mouth as a man grabbed the boy's shoulder and a huge fat woman in turn grabbed the man, shouting in Spanish at him.

The clerk looked at the signature and snapped his fingers. "Linden. Yes, sir, you have a message here."

It was a phone call from Wiley King. In his room Linden placed a call to Raleigh. King described the effects of the molds.

Linden got Reynolds on the phone just as he was entering the museum. Reynolds listened then said, "It's a possibility. A very, distinct possibility. They prefer fungoid growths anyway; maybe they'll eat something that'll kill them. Yes." Reynolds' voice slowly became excited. "It may even be something simple—some strepto-cocci. Good God, Linden, is there any reason why the bacteria shouldn't have enemies too?"

"No, none. They've been as isolated as the insects themselves."

"And some of these bacteria survive fire too. Vacuums, intense cold. . . ." Reynolds started writing quickly. "We'll have to contact the Health Department and get supplies in. This city has every antiviral and antibiotic substance in the world. We'll hit everything—the insects, the eggs. . . ."

"We still haven't cultured any of the *parmiteras'* pathogens."

"We will somehow. We're on to something here, Max."

As usual, Linden tried to call Parmiter and, as usual, the phone was out of order. He hoped it meant that Parmiter was working.

October 3

WITHIN hours after the Mayor of New York City and spokesman for the Department of Agriculture tonelessly announced that *Hephaestus parmitera* was burning up half the country, Montgomery County blossomed with sprinklers, water pails, fire extinguishers, and family members sitting up late at night to keep an eye out for wisps of smoke.

Curing sheds were dampened. Barns were hosed down and dozens of Henry Tacker's neighbors took turns at searching his north pasture, especially where a shiny white concrete slab had sealed the chasm.

That night Jordy Harris' warehouse burned to the ground. It was the only serious damage to the county during the entire plague. The glow from the fire lit up three flat miles of countryside. The hundred or so men who gathered by the road could hear the whirring of the insects from within the flames.

"It's insured," Jordy told everybody, "it's okay. Come on up to the house." He gave his visitors coffee while they set up a poker game in the glare of the fire.

In King's lab every *parmitera* was still and silent in its Petri dish. King took hourly notes on how they fared. None were dead yet, but all were paralyzed.

King talked three times that day to the museum in New York. Linden was guarded but optimistic. The diseases had caused severe attrition of the bead glands. No one had yet cultured the bacteria.

Finally King called Bainboro and bullied Metbaum into forcing Parmiter to the phone. "This idiocy has gone on long enough, Metbaum. Damn it, I want to talk to him."

"You'll be sorry."

Parmiter shouted, "Hello. Is this about your bacteria? You're wasting your time, King."

King said, "They're paralyzed, sir." King realized that he might win the Nobel Prize, inherit a million dollars, or put heaven in a test tube someday, but to Parmiter he would never be anything more than a former student.

"Not for long, King. They're fighting off the antibodies, and they're unfamiliar with certain organisms, but they'll come back."

"How?"

"All they have to do is keep the host alive, not enjoy perfect health. They'll take over all the germs you're shooting into them and use them. They'll be back to normal soon."

King blew up. He was tired and nervous and hopeful, and he was in the midst of an experimental observation which was one of the most exhausting endeavors man had ever dreamed up. He was in the mood for help, not egomania. "Well, I don't think so," he flared. "I think we're on the right track, and even if we aren't, Parmiter, how come we aren't important enough for you to pick up the phone and talk to the human race. . . ." King's outburst ended over what sounded like a bomb going off over the phone.

Parmiter looked down at the smashed remains of the telephone he had just taken apart. Then his enraged face looked up at Metbaum. "Metbaum," he snarled, "don't you ever put me through that again!" He swept the pieces into a trash can. "And get this thing out of here."

The engraved invitation was delivered by a student directly to Parmiter. He was invited to a cocktail party to honor Ernest Jamis, the Director of Development of Bainboro College. Jamis had just financed a soccer field, and Parmiter, being the most famous name among the faculty, was asked to come, in a phrase scrawled at the bottom of the invitation that left no room for escaping. "Expect you five thirty. Do tear yourself away."

Parmiter raged at Metbaum. "Washington is infested with them, just this morning. A national crisis, Metbaum, and I have to tip tiny glasses with stupid women drinking ginger ale. Why! Why!"

Metbaum was carefully arranging a leg muscle of a *parmitera* on a glass slide. He did not look up; nor did he care anymore about Parmiter's rages, which were no longer impressive but now seemed small, mean, and boring. "I don't know, Doc. But I think it'll be good for all of us if you go."

Parmiter's entrance killed the party as usual.

"Why Jim!" said the president's wife, approaching with both arms outstretched.

The other professors nodded curtly and tried to be nice. Like prima donnas, they resented accidental fame.

Parmiter sat stiffly, fiddling with a cup of weak punch, his bow tie pressing his collar against his neck.

The party picked up when champagne was opened to toast Ernest Jamis, the guest of honor. The champagne was withdrawn gingerly from a plastic ice hamper. Gingerly, for the president saw the tiny bubbles inside, sensed the tremendous explosive pressure sealed in the bottle, and did not want the cork to blow the wall out. There was a breathless instant of suspense as he slowly unwound the wire restraining the cork.

Parmiter watched. His eyes fell on the bubbles squashed into flatness by the pressure. Squashed. Parmiter went absolutely slate white. He lowered his glass with shaking hands, eyes riveted to the cork being squeaked free of the bottle.

The bubbles were squashed flat by the pressure. In agony, in agony, the bubbles were in pain . . . agony. . . . A hollow explosion blasted the cork off the wall. The bubbles expanded in relief and boiled upward to the rim of the bottle. Free, free. . . .

Parmiter did not join in the great burst of laughter at the pouring of the champagne. When the president poised the bottle above his glass, he saw the entomologist's eyes—wild, bright, almost mad with growing understanding. "Champagne, James?"

Parmiter shook his head raggedly. He stood shakily. "Pressure," he mumbled.

"In other words, no champagne."

Parmiter looked at the faces looking back at him. "I must apologize. Something just . . . I have to get back to the lab."

An instant's stiffening from all present was the reaction to the small insult. "Tonight you should relax. We appreciate what you're doing about the plague . . . brought credit to the school . . . surely you can relax for an hour. . . ." The president looked at him with growing coolness. "If you must."

There was a general sigh of relief after Parmiter had hurried away. "Friendly fellow," said Hallowell to no one in particular.

Metbaum was in the lab ten minutes after the professor's frantic phone call. He found Parmiter going through the notes of test results gathered over the past week. Some of the papers were scattered on the floor. "Metbaum, did anybody do any tests on atmospheric pressure?"

"Well, at the museum they did something in a vacuum tank. . . ."

"Tests on pressure, Metbaum! Increase it, decrease it. They

didn't, did they!" Parmiter's arm swept toward the shelves with the rustling insects. "It hit me tonight. That's why they're so slow moving! That's why they can't mate!"

"Why?"

"They've got the *bends!* The pressure's killing them. They don't have pressure bladders to relieve it and their carapace is sealed airtight!" Parmiter clasped his hands behind his back and looked around at the insects. "Sea level. Fifteen pounds per square inch. They came from very deep in the earth, Metbaum, remember? I bet if they'd gone upward another thousand feet, some mountain range maybe, they'd have exploded. They cannot depressurize."

"Hold it. If that's true, they'd be like balloons . . ."

". . . or champagne bottles!"

". . . ready to burst at the smallest touch. Why are they so hard to crush?"

Parmiter sat down, rubbing his face. "The shells are supple, not just brittle. Perhaps a foot coming down is too broad a surface; something like a needlepoint would concentrate the pressure . . . or smaller than that."

"But you don't know."

Parmiter's voice slashed out, "I *do* know! I *know*, Metbaum, don't question me!"

"We'll have to call Linden. And Raleigh. . . ."

Metbaum's voice trailed off. Something was happening to Parmiter. Something was wrong with his expression. Parmiter slowly looked up at Metbaum. Then past him, eyes fixed on something behind Metbaum's back. Metbaum whirled around, saw nothing but roach cages. He looked back at Parmiter and was unnerved to find the professor staring straight at him. "I said we'll have to call Linden, Doc. Why are you looking at me like that?"

Parmiter's mouth moved. The single word could have been the dry rustle of an Arctic breeze warning of a storm. "No. We tell no one, Metbaum." He laughed to break the tension. "I could be wrong."

"Me too."

"Didn't mean to scare you, Metbaum." Parmiter stood, voice low, easy, perfectly controlled. He put his hand on Metbaum's shoulder.

"We are on the verge of making fools of ourselves. It may very well not be the pressure after all. You must learn never to rush into things in science, Metbaum. You must state your case and back it up. Evidence. We must have evidence."

Metbaum swallowed an aspirin. He felt a fever coming on. He could not shake the flu. "Yeah."

"We must do an experiment."

"Like what?"

Parmiter's eyes drilled into his. "Metbaum, can you build a pressure tank?"

Metbaum's face lightened. "Oh, sure. Is that all?"

"Quietly? Quickly? Within two days?"

"Why? They've got them in Raleigh. And New York. . . ."

Parmiter's hand tightened on his shoulder. "Metbaum, you don't understand people."

"Yeah?"

"An idea is a possession like any other possession. Like money. It can be stolen. It takes so much work to gain knowledge, Metbaum; it should not be given away lightly."

"People are dying, Doc."

"Thousands more will die if we turn all the resources in the country into chasing after pressure and it turns out we're wrong. Look what's happening with King and his stupid antibiotic spray."

"I thought that was reasonable. Very promising."

"Nonsense, Metbaum. The Museum of Natural History, Raleigh, and half the labs in the country have lost two days already. We must prevent such mistakes. We must do it ourselves. Quietly." Parmiter released Metbaum's shoulder. "Just you and me." Parmiter turned away, voice uncertain. "You don't understand people. Scientists are the worst. One blunder and they're after you forever . . . no peace . . . you've got to protect yourself."

Metbaum felt the lightheaded feeling come back. Odd. He was tired again; he could usually go until five in the morning. He wiped sweat from his face. His thumb ached. "If you *really* believe this is right, Doc. . . ."

"Trust me."

Through the ringing in his ears and the night silences, Metbaum

89

saw the light in Parmiter's eyes. Something warned him that his system was out of kilter; he was not thinking straight. "I'll have to get the materials. Welding equipment. Drills. How big, Doc?"

"Not big, Metbaum. A foot square with a window in it. Not permanent either; just a ball we can pressurize for a week or so. You know machinery and everything; it's your alley, not mine. I'll pay, Metbaum."

"*You'll* pay!"

"I can give you two thousand dollars in the morning. My savings. I'll get it back from the government."

"By when?"

"Two days."

Metbaum looked blearily up at the entomologist. "It seems so sneaky, Doc. Too elaborate."

"Trust me."

"I could go down to New Bern, I guess. How about a diver's helmet?"

"Excellent, Metbaum, excellent."

"We'll need a pump. Oxygen tanks. Hose and a regulator. It'll be goddamn noisy, Doc."

"We'll do it at night. Up here. Just do as I say, Metbaum."

"I always do."

"Trust me, Metbaum."

After Metbaum left, Parmiter sat perfectly still, looking at the cages filled with *parmiteras*. Then he looked at the one item in the lab completely out of place in the racks of glass test tubes and steel shelves. A dirty, scuffed shoebox, taped tightly shut, with air holes punched by a pencil in the top. Madilene's box. His *Gromphadorhina portentosa*—the huge, female Madagascar forest cockroach—made scraping sounds against the cardboard walls of her little prison.

October 4

LIKE a ghost come back to haunt the guilty, the *parmitera* in King's lab that had supposedly died of penicillin mold, unhinged its legs and hoisted its silent body up to full height.

In New York, at the museum, Reynolds and Linden watched the insects come back to life, one by one, and stalk their cages.

King killed and dissected his. The bead glands were now firm, white, and moist.

The first chirping in two days shrieked out of the lab cages. The roaches had recovered from the strongest battery of vaccines, antibiotics, and drugs man could devise. Within hours they were burning wood again.

Linden's phone calls to King were hampered by bad telephone connections. One of the phone junctions between Raleigh and New York had been burned down the previous night. "They just absorbed everything! Reynolds has found penicillin in their systems. They cannot be sterilized."

"What about the sulfa drugs?"

"What about them!"

"Okay. Now what? I'm at my wit's end. I don't even have ideas."

"We're moving into a genuine crisis, King. They say the mayor is going to declare the city a disaster area and try to get spray planes in. They're talking about issuing gas masks to the population."

King felt the tilting, bowel-weakening vertigo he most associated with bad dreams. After all this time he still could not believe it. He laughed or, rather, made a dry rasping sound. "The population of New York City?"

Linden's voice had an edge of fear. "King, you cannot believe what these things are doing! They're still hatching. So far they've killed three hundred people up here. That's just here. They've been blowing up cars all over the place. They've been reported in Ohio. They've got food lines and emergency lines up in the Bronx."

"What are your plans?"

"Back to natural enemies. If we can get some animals to attack the roaches . . . they're going to airlift them from the tropics. . . ."

"Tropics! What kind of animals!"

"I was thinking of centipedes. Or possibly scorpions. Spread them throughout the cities before it gets cold. We've got another two months before winter sets in."

King sat heavily back in his chair and groped for his voice. "I can't believe you're serious."

"Beats gassing them with poison. We'll find out today. Any word from Parmiter?"

King was not listening. Last night one of the campus buildings had burned flat to the ground, and he had been so wrapped up in thoughts of viruses and hope that he had ignored it. He had been to Richmond once this past year. Now he remembered reading that there had been an outbreak of cholera there and that the National Guard had moved in to stop looters. Terror slowly pressed in on him of such bone-chilling depth that he knew he would never lose the memory of it for the rest of his life, never get those blind, flame-throwing, crawling black killers out of his nightmares till he died. "Parmiter? Who knows?"

"Doesn't anybody know what he's doing?"

"He hung up on me yesterday."

"What did he say? Anything?"

King listened to the angry fluttering chirping of the *parmiteras*. "Yes. He said antibiotics were a waste of time." Depression set in on King. He tried to relieve it by hating the dry hard face of Parmiter as it appeared in his memory, but he knew it was himself he hated. "He just said you and I were wasting our time."

"How did he know that? That bastard! Does he. . . ."

"It was just a guess, Doctor. He does this a lot." King looked down at the cages. The phone connection hissed, drowning out Linden's voice and killing it.

King hung up and stretched. He looked at the hundreds of legs surrounding him. He walked into his office and lay down on the couch.

Metbaum clung tightly to the steering wheel and fought down the waves of nausea. He had driven at recklessly mad speed all day, passed three different highway patrol checkpoints to have his car exhaust certified, and arrived on the coast three hours after leaving.

Now he was on his way back to Bainboro. Montgomery County—untouched by fire, even though it was the birthplace of the roaches—flashed by him.

In the trunk of his car were a used diving helmet, a series of pressure gauges, and two-hundred-dollar, gasoline-powered, compressor, escape valves with standard openings, hoses, sealing putty, steel strips with expanding screws, a hand power drill, and several plexiglass sheets.

At five thirty in the afternoon he screeched into the Bainboro quadrangle. Parmiter helped him unload the car and carry the equipment upstairs to the Carson Hall biology lab.

Wiley King awoke at eight o'clock. He checked the samples, then got in his car and drove home. He had a TV dinner, then watched a newscaster say that as of nine o'clock that evening more than a thousand people had died on the Eastern Seaboard from the Hephaestus Plague.

October 5

THE school awoke at eight in the morning, with students hurrying to classes and breakfast.

Parmiter awoke from his slumber on his desk, with his right arm numbed from the weight of his head. He saw Metbaum still feverishly working in the lab. He brought three aspirins to him for breakfast. "How long, Metbaum?"

The student said, "This afternoon, I think." He drilled neatly, placing holes for hose couplings.

A fire that morning had damaged the generator plant serving the museum, so they were forced to watch the fight between the centipede and the *parmitera* in partial dimness.

The centipede had been removed from an earth-filled case where it had been nestling tightly beneath a rock. It had been dropped gingerly into the bare arena—an emptied snake box with a transparent top and side where it scurried nervously about looking for something to nestle under. The centipede would have paced until it literally died of exhaustion. For reasons still unclear, the creature was never comfortable unless both its belly and its back touched something simultaneously. A bare box without rocks or leaves or twigs was a death trap. So when the *parmitera* was dropped in, the centipede rushed it, snatched it in its poison-tipped legs, curled its fanlike body in a constrictive death grip, and savagely bit at the roach's case.

Forty-five minutes later the centipede—eyes destroyed, legs scattered about the cage, jaws torn and fractured, and body burned—lay on its back and was torn apart by the roach's digging legs and whirring cerci.

They tried a scorpion. The roach chewed ash as the stinger bounced off its shell. The scientists rescued the scorpion just as the roach finished eating and began showing signs of annoyance.

Neither of those two animals could have been turned loose in populated areas even if they had been able to kill the roach. But their use illustrated the growing desperation that even Linden shared to find something, *anything*, that would kill the roaches.

For an hour the biologists went a little crazy. They unleashed every animal they could think of against the roaches while the city burned outside. Cats. Rats. Dogs. Toucans. Hawks. Parrots. Armadillos. Baboon spiders. Chimpanzees. Falcons. And one Gila monster that gulped down a *parmitera* whole, then thrashed in agony as the insect burned through its stomach and ribs, emerging bloody but unscathed from the lizard's back.

At seven that evening one of the biologists reported success of a sort. "I dropped one into a jar of pure sulfuric acid. It died."

Linden looked quietly around at the men seated at the table. "Does anybody know if it sheds its skeleton? Does it molt?"

Reynolds said, "Maybe. But they'd have to be older, I guess. None of them have died of age yet."

"They do not have a metamorphosis stage. The eggs are as armored in their container as the bodies. They're still hatching too." Linden picked up a sheet of paper with the mayor's seal visible on the letterhead. "We have been asked for comments on a contingency plan that the government has drawn up in case of things getting hopeless. It calls for massive dispersals of DDT, endrin, parathion, Paris green, and nicotine sulfate by extermination units. The public will be equipped with protective masks and the doses will be carefully set up, building by building. It mentions evacuations of blocks and everything."

Reynolds said flatly, "No. We'd poison the planet. The amounts required are too large." The others concurred.

"Then it's back to pathology. Find an antibiotic that kills the bacteria. *Hephaestus parmitera* has plenty of natural enemies, but none can kill it." Linden avoided their eyes after he had said this. No one, as far as they knew, had ever heard of a cure for a pathogen that had never been cultured.

They returned to the lab. Linden was bitten by the coral snake as he was closing the sliding door to the cage. The jaws clamped to the heel of his hand. Linden gently disengaged the snake's jaws, placing the snake in the cage, and called Reynolds.

When Reynolds got to him, Linden's hand was swelling. The entomologist sagged as a needle full of antivenin slipped into his arm. Reynolds latched the door to the snake's cage, then kneeled with his hand on Linden's pulse until the ambulance arrived.

In the hospital Linden opened his eyes and saw the blurred features of Reynolds. "Stupid thing."

"You had shock there for a moment. They gave you the antivenin in time." Reynolds was talking about the bodily shock caused by venom. The fluid injected into Linden's arm, the antivenin, had blocked the poison, but Linden was extremely weak.

"Good thing it wasn't that cobra, Doc."

Linden closed his eyes. Reynolds thought he had dropped off to sleep. He was about to leave when he heard Linden whisper between cracked lips, "Parmiter . . ."

Reynolds said, "No, I'm Reynolds." He spoke slowly and clearly. "You're getting delirious. . . ."

Linden frowned and shook his head on the pillow. "No . . . the fire engines . . . fire engines. . . ."

"What about the fire engines?"

"Tell . . . Parmiter . . . the fires. . . ." Linden yawned in midsentence. He exhaled slowly and dropped off to sleep. In repose

95

Linden looked very old. It was some moments before Reynolds realized that Linden wanted somebody to tell Parmiter about the half hour cycles of fires.

Afternoon light faded once again into twilight across Bainboro. Metbaum worked on. Students returned home. Some went to the Student Union for a scheduled dance, and the sounds of rock music floated into the lab. At eight thirty, twenty-six straight hours after he had begun, Metbaum straightened up painfully and looked at his handiwork.

Layers of steel and plexiglass sealed the neck opening of the helmet. Pressure and gas gauges protruded from the top. A line snaked across the floor to the heavy air compressor. The helmet coupling was pressure tight and could be removed and resealed without loss of pressure.

Metbaum gulped down vitamins and a fruit bar. He had a fever, a bad one. His head swam. He staggered to Parmiter's office door and saw the professor sitting in the chair, eyes looking at the wall. Thinking.

Metbaum leaned for support against the doorjamb. "Let's go, Doc. It's ready."

Parmiter did not move.

"Come on, Doc, what's wrong?"

"Eh? Wrong?" Parmiter looked at him. "Nothing's wrong, Metbaum. I'm memorizing the lab, that's all. I want to remember tonight."

The compressor clattered and roared thunderously in the small lab, startling the *parmiteras*. Parmiter nervously opened the faceplate of the helmet and inserted small saucers containing water, cracker crumbs, crumpled paste, and a bowl of fine ash. He found a male *parmitera* and placed it inside also.

Then from the shoebox Parmiter tenderly lifted Madilene. Holding her in the palm of his hand as though she were precious water, Parmiter placed her inside the bowl of cracker crumbs.

Metbaum shouted, "Hey!"

Parmiter ignored him over the roar of the compressor. He closed the faceplate, latched it, then spun around in shock as Metbaum's hand grabbed his shoulder.

"What the hell's *she* doing in there!"

"Company. Turn your dials, Metbaum."

"My ass!" Metbaum's face worked in concentration, then light flooded into his flushed features. "My God!"

"What!"

"You bastard! You bastard, Parmiter, you're trying to *breed* these things!"

"Metbaum, I'm trying to make them copulate! That's the only way we can tell if pressure's what's wrong with them. I insist you stop arguing and make this thing work!"

"To hell with that! You'll have a new strain! Another generation!"

"Trust me, Metbaum."

Metbaum looked wildly from the professor to the tank and back again. Then he flung an empty beaker at the compressor, where it smashed into glittering glass splinters.

Parmiter said, "Since you've already spent considerable effort and brainpower designing this thing, Metbaum, we may as well see how it works. Stop being a child and let's get going."

Metbaum sat heavily on the bench, then forced himself to his feet again and went over to the compressor. He leaned against it and muttered something to himself.

"What?" asked Parmiter.

"What's the use? Go ahead."

As the pressure bled in, Parmiter closely watched both bugs. Madilene felt the atmosphere change immediately and her body tissues adjusted to it. She froze, the antennae stiffened, questioning the air flowing in, and the growing weight caused an accelerated contraction and expansion of her shell.

The male remained motionless up to where the gauge read ninety pounds per square inch. Then his multiarticulated legs raised his bulbous body up to an aggressive springing posture. He extended one foreleg, searching for a foothole in the smooth metal.

"Easy, Metbaum," Parmiter shouted. "It's working."

The pressure rose steadily. Parmiter's pounding heart forced sweat onto his forehead. He wiped it with his sleeve.

Madilene clambered around the tank, checking out the hose couplings and crevices. Then in a burst of mindless rage, she raced up to the male and dug furiously at his body with one leg. Just as rapidly she lost interest in him and nervously skittered around the circumference of her prison.

The pressure touched one hundred and thirty-four pounds. For one breathless second it seemed as though the male had gathered together all the unnatural power accumulated by his weeks of pain. He stiffened and then contracted his shell, violently squeezing out the pressure in his body. His legs pushed at the floor of the tank. Then he disappeared before Parmiter's eyes.

"Cut it off, Metbaum!"

Madilene flashed to the spot where the male had just been. Her mouth was open and Parmiter could hear her hiss. Parmiter bent down to look at the roof of the tank. The male was nestled against a screened hose coupling.

"God almighty," breathed Parmiter.

"What's happening?" Metbaum shouted.

"Come and look!" Parmiter tapped the top of the tank, but the male did not budge.

Madilene hissed up at the black roach. That got him moving. He climbed down from the roof. He did not walk so much as descend, a miniature black thundercloud floating down as inexorably as oil. On the floor he faced Madilene. Madilene backed away from him, hissing angrily. Her antennae reached out toward him. And with unspeakable savagery, the male sprang for her.

Parmiter cried out in horror and pounded the tank. Metbaum knelt down beside him and peered in.

Madilene grasped the *parmitera* around the lower edge of his carapace in her jaws. He wrenched her violently back and forth like a lion shaking loose a hyena. Both men could hear the scrape of their bodies in the tank.

To slow down the *parmitera*'s twisting, Madilene wrapped her legs around him, climbed halfway onto his back, and began biting in earnest. It was useless against his armored back.

One of her mouth parts got caught in his leg. It stuck fast, and instantly her advantage was lost. The male chirped and flipped onto his back, snapping off her mandible. Madilene quit the fight and retreated to a corner. And the *parmitera* executed a move so seemingly human that Parmiter and Metbaum looked at each other simultaneously.

He rocked from side to side on his rounded back. At the point at which he would have upended himself like a turtle rolling onto his feet, the bug stalled. A leg shot out, gripped the floor, and pushed his body onto his feet like a wrestler rolling onto his stomach, taking a deep breath, and pushing himself to his feet with his arms.

"Still sorry I put her in there, Metbaum?" asked Parmiter as they straightened up.

Metbaum stared down at the tank. He was obviously repulsed by Parmiter's manipulations, but he was also fascinated by the two insects. Possibilities gripped his imagination so strongly that he did not get angry with Parmiter as he instinctively thought he should. It was no longer possible. He was caught up in it.

He looked up at Parmiter and played uncertainly with his thumb bandage again. He felt as if he had been soundly beaten in some challenge he forgot he had accepted. He tried to speak, but already Parmiter had forgotten about him, ignored his presence as he gathered together his notes and began uncoupling the hoses the way Metbaum had shown him earlier. Metbaum looked out the big picture windows of the lab.

"Go home, Metbaum. Sleep all day."

Metbaum slowly, unsteadily, gathered up his notes and walked out.

Parmiter gazed raptly at the *parmitera* behind the glass. He whispered gently to the glass, "Your name is Clarence. Clarence. I had a cocker spaniel named that once. Once when I was young. I loved it, but it died. You will not die."

The last pink wisp of moon was blackened by clouds. It was pitch black outside, the dead of night.

October 6

AT four in the morning Gerald Metbaum awakened from a deep, sweaty sleep and attempted to strangle his girlfriend lying in bed next to him. She screamed and rolled free.

In a frenzy of uncoordinated jerky motion, Metbaum ran to the wall and screamed and pounded on it till his wrists were swollen. Then he collapsed on the floor. He babbled about fires with legs coming to eat him.

The intern in the ambulance recognized the symptoms of delirium and sedated him. Metbaum's left arm was swollen to the size of an oak branch, with violent red streaks emanating from a bandage on his thumb.

"One of those bugs bit him!" the girlfriend sobbed. "I told him he should have told somebody!"

"Did he treat it?"

"Iodine! He put on all that iodine and one goddamned Band-Aid!"

In the hospital they packed him in ice to break his hundred-and-five-degree fever.

A student ran into Carson Hall to tell Parmiter but found it deserted. He then drove to the entomologist's house on Summit Avenue and was surprised to find the professor wide awake and unshaven.

Parmiter's face betrayed no emotion at the news, even at the fact that Metbaum had been bitten by a roach. He called the hospital.

A doctor said, "He went into coma at six this morning. It's a damned odd infection. White blood cell and red blood cell counts are proportionally normal. The thing is there's more of everything in his bloodstream, as if he's so overnourished his whole system is clogging. There's pus in the wound but no real gangrene. We just have to wait it out."

"Listen, Doctor, take a pint of his blood and hold it. You'll be receiving a call from the Board of Health."

Parmiter took a deep breath and, with the hated telephone clutched tightly in his hand, dialed Wiley King in Raleigh. His voice overrode King's apologies. "Send someone over to Memorial Hospital in Bainboro to pick up some blood."

"Some what?"

"*Blood*, King! We've finally cultured the *parmitera*'s bacteria. The medium is human blood."

He heard the scratch of a pen over the line. "Oh, boy. Oh, boy," muttered King. "I wish Linden could have heard this."

"Precisely what does that mean, King?"

"You don't answer your phone so you wouldn't know. A lab snake bit him. He's in the hospital. He's okay, but he'll be out of it for a couple months . . . Oh damn, he had a message for you."

"What message!"

"Hold the line, I want to get this to the Health Department." The line went dead. Parmiter waited, then King's voice came back. "He wanted you to know the New York Fire Department learned that the fires are sometimes cyclical. Half an hour after fires are reported, they spring up again. They found it's the same in Washington and Richmond. Something makes the roaches start another fire as soon as they've got one going. Usually they're all clustered together. What do you make of that?"

It triggered a boulder of a thought in Parmiter's mind that would not quite make itself felt. Pressure. Pressure change? Impossible.

"I don't know," he said at last, "but it's important."

"How do you know?"

"Damn it, I *know*!" Parmiter raged, sick and tired at having to repeat what he assumed was obvious to everybody by now.

In the murky, musty basement on a card table recently cleared of rubbish lay the helmet. A single tensor lamp shined through the faceplate, illuminating the inside of the helmet. The compressor stood in the corner. Parmiter had managed to get it home at 4 A.M. Parmiter's basement was damp and cold, even in summer. A naked bulb hung from the ceiling by a string wire, and the only entrance was down a set of creaking, wooden stairs from the living room.

The corners were cluttered with cardboard cartons, stuffed with moldering papers and yearbooks, letters, old magazines—some with articles he had written in those happy days when he was writing—and junk he had picked up out of curiosity—old maps, a rusty carburetor, a television tube. The basement was quiet. *Thank God, peace and quiet!*

Clarence and Madilene muddled about in a welter of ash and cracker crumbs. Parmiter was dismayed to see the glass fogging on the inside a bit from the bowl of water. He carefully ran a lighted match across the surface of the glass. The fog diluted to crystalline droplets that ran down the glass.

Now he could clearly see the two insects. They were motionless. Parmiter rested his chin in his hand. For fifteen minutes he watched them without moving. Then he spoke. "I wonder if you can feel me out here. I want you to sense my presence. I will become as fixed a part of your lives as those food bowls."

No movement answered him. Nothing. But he was not discouraged.

In the lab Parmiter restlessly gathered together the tape cassettes and looked around for the container for them. Without Metbaum he could not find anything in the place, could not even remember his own ideas without somebody to feed them back to him. He had not been without an assistant for years.

The fire engines. Parmiter opened and shut a couple of cages. His blood pressure was up. The idea would not come forth. He sat on the bench and clutched his head in his hands. Then because he was deafened by the silence he turned on Metbaum's transistor radio, which lay forlornly on the table.

Parmiter went through all his sheets on the *parmiteras*, searching for some clue to the fire cycles. Food? No, still the pressure, something to do with the pressure. Pain. What caused it?

Divers who rise too fast collect nitrogen bubbles in the blood causing indescribable agony. The nitrogen becomes bubbles because the body did not have time to absorb it. The bubbles appeared because of pressure, boiling out . . . surging like champagne. . . .

Parmiter doodled little bombs and arrows on a scratch pad. Pressure.

From across the hall came the mad shrieking of the *parmiteras*.

They had been screaming in agony for a full minute before Parmiter noticed them. He looked at the maddened insects in astonishment.

Almost every one was clinging to its cage trying to burn itself free. Six were on their backs, sawing at the air. Parmiter caught three that had escaped. They burned his hand as he tossed them back into their prisons. He looked frantically around. His entire sample collection was dying in front of his eyes.

As his eyes traversed from cage to cage across the lab, something off-center caught his attention. Metbaum's radio. The shrieks were so loud that they drowned out its sound. As Parmiter bent over to listen, he heard only static with a low underwhine. He cut off the sound.

As the wind dies away in branches, leaving only scattered flutters of leaves, the shrieks of the *parmiteras* died slowly away leaving only an isolated click or two.

Parmiter transferred all but one roach out of a cage. He carried the cage into his office along with the radio. He turned on the radio and found more static with that same low whine. He placed the radio in the cage with the bug and turned the volume on full. The *parmitera* attacked the radio, legs scrabbling ferociously at the speaker, cerci whirring frantically.

After several seconds the insect flipped onto its back. Its legs writhed, then it became still. Parmiter picked it up. The shell was crinkly and soft, crisscrossed into a thousand intersecting cracks. He dissected it. The tissues had been blasted to a pulp. The roach looked as if it were filled with hamburger.

The answer clicked into place in his mind.

Sound waves. Like millions of needles of molecular width striking millions of balloons and exploding them, ultrasonic waves assaulted those iron shells in tidal furies, straining the already stressed bodies to the bursting point.

Basic physics stated that the smaller the contact surface between two objects, the greater the pressure. Two hundred pounds of pressure concentrated on a bootsole had to be applied repeatedly to crush one roach. The needle of a centipede fang under full strength could not break through. But ultrasonic waves were thinner than any needle. At frequencies too high for humans to hear, sound waves were deadly. They could cut steel and drill teeth. And their razor impact literally tore the molecular structure of the roach shells apart.

The expression of uncertainty on Parmiter's face rearranged itself into the tight, controlled haughty look that was customary for him. He wrote notes. He tested various effects of different types of sound on the roaches.

It was the fire sirens that had caused the half hour cycles of flame. Intense enough to enrage to flaming agony but not intense enough to kill, the approaching sirens maddened the roaches lurking in the buildings to where the fires spread every time an alarm was turned in.

Since Parmiter's office phone was still unworkable, he went down to Hallowell's office and dialed Raleigh.

"Doctor King, take notes. This is important. The roaches are under intense internal pressure and unable to relieve it sufficiently to breed. I have determined the exact amount of pressure within them as well as a guess at the type of sound waves necessary to kill them. . . ."

"*Kill* them! Hold the phone. . . ."

"I will *not*, King! I will say it once more. The insects can be killed by the application of sound waves. . . ."

Within three hours the information had gone out to every university studying the roaches. Confirmation poured into the Department of Agriculture, for the rest of the day.

At the Museum of Natural History Reynolds placed a roach before a public address speaker and passed the microphone in front of it, causing a feedback blare. The insect exploded.

By six that night sound experts at the Museum of Natural History and the Department of Agriculture had determined the exact frequency that would kill the roaches and the exact minimum and maximum distances needed to make a feasible weapon.

Reynolds dropped flowers into the vase next to Linden. "Push the decibel tolerance any further and you'll be killing people. Push it any less and the roaches will make more fires. It all has to be fairly exact. I know it's not perfect by a damn sight but. . . ." Reynolds smiled.

Linden's eyes were still wracked with pain, but interest made them alive. He listened but did not speak, and Reynolds didn't encourage him to. There was nothing to say.

"It's so simple that anybody with a stereo player and speakers can cross wires and kill them. The government is underwriting the cost of speaker banks on patrol cars and two-man extermination units."

Far down on the street the crackling fire of the four-story building was silenced by the thickness of the windowglass. Like any fire engine chaser, Reynolds watched the trucks unroll hoses and direct the streams of water. "The city has killed all sirens and is going to impound transistor radios. Parmiter did it. Parmiter was right."

Linden smiled. Then his eyes drooped. His old dry lips puckered and relaxed. He was asleep and did not hear Reynolds' last words. "I believe, sir, we're on the winning side."

Within the next two months the plague would kill hundreds more people trapped late at night in suddenly flaming homes or blown to gas-soaked particles by exploding automobiles. Even Reynolds would have admitted much later that despite the discovery of the sound waves, the worst was yet to come.

But when he went home that night, when the Department of Agriculture closed its doors and Wiley King got his first decent night's sleep, a series of events that would—if they ever became known—represent the greatest advance in biology in the twentieth century was well under way, an event that made the plague seem like a minor zephyr in a world of potential tornadoes.

None of the people who had known him—neither Max Linden, nor Metbaum, nor King, nor even his colleagues at Bainboro—would have been surprised to learn that the new Darwin or Linnaeus or William Harvey was to be the frail, snappish man named James Lang Parmiter. Deep in his rank basement, cut off from humanity at large, the Bainboro entomologist playing with his nervous insects had enough eccentricity for greatness. But even he himself did not suspect this until the following day when the roaches still raged through the cities of the country, burning cities and towns and woods at an even more desperate rate.

Parmiter knew the reporters would be back in full force. On his basement cot he mapped out his route to the school with customary thoroughness. When he arrived at Carson Hall the following morning, a package was waiting on his desk. It had been sent from a pathology lab in Raleigh and described the genetic makeup of *Hephaestus parmitera*.

Part 2

WINTER

November

THE photographs showed chains of fuzzy balls on a limbo background. Parmiter read the attached reports. The information had been sent by Wiley King, and it detailed the results of electron miscroscope studies of the genetic structures found in the saliva of *Hephaestus parmitera*.

One of the first things that Parmiter told his classes was that *Drosophila*, the common fruit fly, had four pairs of chromosomes so clearly defined that they were ideal for laboratory study. The chromosome count held true for nearly all insects. However, it was not true for *Hephaestus parmitera*. The roaches had seventeen pairs. Human beings had forty-eight chromosomes. Twenty-four pairs.

Contained within the chromosome chains were the genetic possibilities that determined the structure of an animal. Seventeen pairs of chromosomes shown to a scientist without telling him where they had come from would convince him that the organism was at least a primate. Certainly not an insect. The genetic count alone made Parmiter exultant. It confirmed what he had suspected after learning that the roaches could survive off pure carbon. The roaches had the greatest potential for mutation of any insect in existence.

The night Parmiter had set up the pressure tank in the basement, Madilene and Clarence had begun a dance with each other, as slow, suggestive, and graceful a ballet as any human passion could express. Facing each other, antennae waving like seaweed in a river current, the two insects circled slowly in the tank. Parmiter, sitting on the edge of his cot, wrote down every movement they made.

Like the common German roach, Clarence tried to slide under Madilene's belly to present the pheromones on his back for her tongue. Like the Madeira roach, Clarence danced to seduce the female by hypnotism. Blindness was something he did not know he had; millions of generations had made sight useless for him.

Parmiter tiptoed over from the cot. He turned on a tensor lamp, shining it directly into the faceplate. The roaches paused immediately. This told Parmiter something else. Without eyes, Clarence sensed light. Madilene must have sensed Parmiter's presence, too. They did not move during the rest of the night.

During the next several days, Parmiter's basement came to resemble a prison cell. A chest of drawers held his clothes. An old Army cot was moved down from the attic. He propped a small woman's compact mirror over the laundry sink to shave by.

Parmiter left the house only for classes. He noted various effects of the plague around Bainboro and forgot them immediately. Slender poles with speakers nestled in the campus shrubbery. Police cars added speakers to the roof and sides of buildings, disguising the speakers to make them look like machines with strange exotic flower petals.

The plague was worse than ever and it was a measure of his distraction that Parmiter did not notice certain unpleasant things. Smoke in the air. Spectacular sunsets caused by the presence of smoke in the atmosphere from the city fires, much like the effects seen during the dust bowl days. The speakers were a declaration of war for the roaches, one that was doomed to destroy them, and they were going down in fury. A house burned on Forest Avenue down the block from Parmiter, and he did not know about it for a week.

After a lunch in the cafeteria of milk and salad, Parmiter hurried home to lock himself away in the dark basement. Naturally the phone was unplugged. Without knowing when it had actually begun, Parmiter found himself talking to the insects. He knew voice vibrations would be picked up inside the tank. And he told them that fact. "The sound waves from my voice are hitting your shells. I want you to get used to them. I will become part of your environment; normal, everyday facts of your life will include me. You're in my basement in a tank I have given you. Can you hear me? Understand me? No, of course not. It is just my voice you hear, not my words. I have patience though. Infinite patience."

Sometimes Parmiter was afraid of some of the things he said to them. "I have no friends. Emotion is so dangerous except when its purposes are well defined as they are in your world. We should be closer to your world. Or else you should be closer to ours. We must learn to understand emotions. Perhaps we can share them."

Once, when eating a sandwich, Parmiter said, "I have no one else. I want no one else. We must help each other. . . ." Then he stopped. He wondered if this was how people went crazy, by enjoying themselves too much, by indulging a small habit which turned out to be not only very big, but too big to see in perspective.

When Parmiter looked into the helmet, he grasped the edge of the table in delight. Crazy or not, whatever he was doing was working well. In the center of the helmet lay a small, moist, brown parcel resembling a badly wrapped package. Clarence and Madilene avoided it. An egg case.

One morning Gerald Metbaum's eyes vibrated and opened. He looked around the white-walled room and tried to get out of bed. His forearm was as thin as a crowbar. When he saw it, Metbaum realized he was in a hospital.

When Parmiter arrived, the student was sitting up eating a plate of scrambled eggs. "Hi, Doc!" For just an instant Metbaum's eyes took in the incredible fact that Parmiter needed a shave.

"You're looking chipper, Metbaum. Are you all right?"

"I feel great." Metbaum pushed the plate farther down on the bed. It seemed heavy to him. "What's been happening?"

"I guess you've heard about the sound waves."

"Some doctor explained it to me. He said you learned it."

"That's right, that's right. They're a mixed blessing, I'm afraid. It's difficult to get frequency and distance perfect. You wind up making them mad just as often as you kill them." Parmiter described Washington. Richmond. The National Guard. Looting. The South was still relatively safe, except for the forests.

"What's going to happen?" asked Metbaum.

"Winter. And enough extermination units. It's been raining pretty heavily all over here, which is a blessing. But it will take time."

"How many people . . ."

"Last I heard three or four thousand." Parmiter balanced the umbrella tip on the floor by pressing on the handle with his hand, as he sat in a chair.

"Sound waves," muttered Metbaum.

Parmiter described Linden's snake bite. "They flew him back home. He'll be okay."

"When did you talk to him?"

Parmiter said, "I haven't had a chance yet . . . actually . . ."

Metbaum waved a hand. "Shit. You don't have to do anything, Doc. What about that pressure tank?"

"You can have the parts if you want them. It's at my . . ."

"No, I mean what happened with the roaches!"

"Nothing."

"Nothing?"

"Both of them died."

"Without mating?"

"Yes."

Metbaum exhaled slowly.

Parmiter looked down at his umbrella as if it fascinated him. "Are you glad?"

"Don't be obvious, Doc."

"They have as much right as anything to live."

"No, they don't."

"Oh?"

"They kill people."

"That's not the point, is it, Metbaum?"

"If it isn't, I'd like to know what is."

"They remind us we don't own the earth."

"Neither do they."

"Well, we're acting as if we do, Metbaum!"

"So are they!" Metbaum looked at Parmiter lazily. "Even as a biologist, Doc, you know they're not worth saving considering what they do . . . Oh, the hell with it."

"Will you be all right, Metbaum?"

"I will eventually. Don't know when though." Metbaum's eyes dropped, then closed. He seemed to have fallen asleep. As Parmiter rose, Metbaum's eyes opened again. His voice was clogged and dim. "You need a bath," he muttered.

"I *what?*"

"You don't smell too good." The voice blurred to the edge of incoherence. "You're falling apart, Doc; you look like hell. You ought to change that suit, man. You're . . . sure wish . . . just sit and think except you get tired . . . tired. . . ."

That Metbaum was ill when he said it did not placate Parmiter. Still scandalized by what he considered a personal insult, he stalked out the door and slammed it shut.

Parmiter unscrewed the tank valve and listened to the hiss of escaping air as the pressure drained away. "Hang on, Clarence," he said to the tank. "Pain time again. Sorry." Clarence emitted a single chirp and bumped Parmiter's glove as it touched the eggs.

When Parmiter reached for them again, Clarence covered the entire egg case with his body. His carapace rippled slightly. Parmiter glimpsed the tongue washing over the eggs. Clarence was protecting them. The male of the species was protecting the eggs.

Madilene's instincts had been scrambled by her captivity and rather than bury the eggs, she had dropped the egg case on the floor of her prison. Roaches did not lay eggs by the thousands as flies did. They laid a case containing less than twenty and carried them around until the young could fend for themselves. These creatures were different. They exhibited solicitude.

Madilene remained in her corner as Clarence lumbered about under the decreasing pressure. He picked the eggs up and carried them around in his mouth. Parmiter could tell by its texture that the case was not the bullet-hard container hatched by the other *parmiteras*. Then, as Parmiter looked closer, he realized what Clarence was actually doing. The roach was transferring bacteria to the young while they were still gestating, just as Linden had described. It was like bees feeding predigested food to their offspring.

Parmiter tried to slip his glove under Clarence, but the bug was not having any of it. He chirped and raged and raised so much hell that the entomologist gave up. He decided to leave Madilene in the helmet and fix up a small vivarium for Clarence. Dirt was arranged in small hillocks with a saucer of water worked into the landscape. He put it on the worktable and closed its top with wire mesh. Clarence's new home.

At that time the egg case had grown to the size of a peanut, and Clarence jealously guarded it, even after being transferred to the vivarium. Every time Parmiter reached for the eggs, Clarence chirped loudly. The pressure change caused by the forced removal from the tank had slowed him down to where he laboriously bumped about in the vivarium or lay quietly at the bottom.

Every day at six ten exactly Parmiter placed a bowl of ash into the vivarium. To reinforce his routine, he said, "Good evening, Clarence."

Since the rest of Parmiter's house had gathered a layer of dust, he had a maid in one day to clean it. The cleaning had taken seven hours, and Parmiter hovered ghostlike around the maid. The woman finally burst into tears and flung down her mop. Parmiter paid her off. That night, as usual, he locked all the doors and went down to the basement to sleep with the insects.

The events that began that night piled in with such paralyzing suddenness that Parmiter nearly lost sense of time. The days ran together connected only by events that scorched his memory. Clarence began a series of games with him. The more he thought about it the more Parmiter decided they had started at two o'clock that morning.

At three in the morning, Parmiter awoke in a cold, shivering sweat. Not moving, he lay in the cot, listening to the drip of cold water through the pipes. Parmiter knew the basement was cold by the chill on the dark silent air. Somebody was in the house upstairs.

Careful now. Get the light on. Wait a minute; you know where they are—you can feel them! Parmiter snapped on the bedside tensor. The feeble light tugged helplessly at the darkest crevices of the basement. *The bedroom! The bedroom!*

"Who's there?" Parmiter cried. His voice died without making a dent in the blanket of darkness.

A sound. A single loud chirp from upstairs. Parmiter sprang from the cot and put on the vivarium light. The egg case was there. But Clarence was gone.

He ran barefoot over the cold stone floor up to the kitchen where he turned on the fluorescent light. Soft, white light flooded the room. Parmiter looked carefully, for the roach could have been anywhere. Baseboard. Sink. Food cabinet. Refrigerator.

Above the sink was a small window with a crank handle. It opened over the backyard. The window was slightly ajar and cold air weaved in through it. Clarence was crouched down against the sill. He chirped. The roach let Parmiter pick him up and carry him back to the basement.

An edge of the screen covering the vivarium was bent. Clarence had escaped through the hole. Parmiter wrapped a second layer of screen over the top. Then he went back to bed.

Clarence escaped again the next day, burning his way through the cheap, soft tin screen while Parmiter was at the laundry. The minute Parmiter pulled out his front door key he had the feeling again that somebody had invaded his house. He set the laundry down in the living room. He smelled smoke in the air. On the linoleum floor of the kitchen were two small burned spots.

Parmiter tore the paper wrapping off the laundry and feverishly dropped it into the sink. He set it afire. A blaze of flame welled up and puffed the paper into ashes. Parmiter coughed at the acrid smell as he gathered the ashes up and sprinkled them over the freshly vacuumed living room rug. He sat on the sofa and listened.

A clock ticked in the kitchen. And from within the bedroom Parmiter heard a faint scratching. Clarence was on the sill of the bedroom window, the big one with a storm lining. He had been climbing down to get to the ash smell when Parmiter scooped him up. When Parmiter dropped him into the vivarium, he noticed that the egg case was vibrating slightly.

More layers of screen went over the top of the vivarium, all week long. Each time Clarence burned his way out. Wednesday Parmiter laid a sheet of steel over the top. Clarence beat himself against it so violently that Parmiter immediately took it off. He sat in the basement and turned out the lights. He watched Clarence. "What's got into you? If I let you roam around, you'll disappear on me! Or will you?"

Clarence remained in the tank. He would not leave if Parmiter was there.

Each morning Parmiter checked the bowl. He stopped trying to confine the bug now. Each day when he returned, Clarence would be loose in the house and there would be a new burned spot somewhere. The bathtub drain. The front door transom. A closet. Once in the attic. Always the bug would greet him with a chirp and let himself be carried downstairs to the basement. He never went alone.

Clarence obviously considered Parmiter part of his surroundings. He never chirped at him except to call attention to himself.

One day Parmiter broke the routine. He came home with a sack of groceries and found Clarence in the bedroom again. The bug chirped at him. Parmiter ignored it. He stacked food in his refrigerator. Clarence chirped again insistently, then again. Finally a long sawing series of chirps that scorched the curtain broke out. Parmiter called, "I'm coming!" At the sound of Parmiter's voice, Clarence shut up.

Parmiter added notes to his log about the bug's odd behavior. It was connected with the terminating development of the eggs. By deserting them for long periods of time Clarence revealed that they were about to hatch. And each time he found Clarence in the house, the roach was close to an exit. A window or a door crack.

Clarence arranged his activities around Parmiter. He recognized him and waited for him each day. An empathy had been established between them.

On the basis alone of Clarence's extraordinary behavior Parmiter could easily have gotten funds to stop teaching and devote all his time to Clarence. It would have indeed made Parmiter famous. He could write a book. He could teach anywhere. If Clarence died tomorrow, Parmiter could be set for life.

But getting a grant would take time. He would have to leave the bug. He would have to fill out forms, present his evidence, wait for responses from strange, critical people. Parmiter did not want to be famous. He did not want to talk on phones to strangers and endure their fatuous compliments. He did not want to break this fragile routine. He liked what was happening and wanted to see how it would end.

He peered at the egg case. It was half as big as Clarence himself. It shivered constantly and was covered with a moist film.

One day Parmiter came home and found Clarence in the vivarium where he had left him that morning. "What's up, boy?" asked Parmiter. "You don't like traveling anymore?"

Clarence remained in the same position. He was watching the egg case.

Parmiter went to bed that night and had a nightmare. In the dark sea his mother's face was slowly transmuted. The eyes swelled toward a faceted blankness, and the first buds of antennae pulsed in her forehead. Her hands and arms became thin and a shell appeared over them. It was straining . . . straining. . . .

Parmiter woke up shouting in an ecstasy of horror, staggered out of bed, and walked unsteadily to the door. Halfway there he vomited. Upstairs, he poured a slug of brandy and waited for his heart to slow down. It was freezing in that basement; he should bring more blankets down. He rubbed his eyes. The nightmare had a feel of inevitability to it.

His mind had been working hard on the speculations about the egg case and what kind of creatures would emerge from it. These thoughts had invaded another secret part of his mind, where he stored faces of most people and brought them forth from time to time. He had confused his fantasies. He remained awake the rest of the night, looking at the egg case. He stood by the egg case. He knew he should examine the glittering packet, that dark, damp gem lying before Clarence. He should get in there closer somehow. He was missing an opportunity.

The next day Parmiter was sick. The nerves of his body grated against the bones. His hands shook constantly and he was nauseated. His senses betrayed him. The bright colors of the town jabbed and drilled at his optic nerves. Sounds made his skin crawl. Tension knotted the organs of his body. He dismissed his seminar early. One of the students asked if he was well and Parmiter screeched an answer back.

He went home. He dreaded sleep, for he knew the frightening forms would rise again. He sat in the basement, eyes blinking rapidly until he could no longer sit staring at the roach without moving, just as it stared at the eggs. Night came. Dark arose. Parmiter fought sleep. The shapes welled up so heavily his head drooped down, his strength melted, and he collapsed back on the bed.

That night it happened again. Fear. Horror. Strange shapes and night creatures, and suddenly Parmiter was looking at the long string dangling down from the basement light fixture. He watched it for some time, not sure he had really been sleeping but certain that he was awake and alive in his basement and that things were normal.

Parmiter smelled the cold stone and dust of the basement. He put on the tensor with the cable switch. Under the lamp the vivarium was empty. Clarence was gone. He had taken the egg case with him.

Henry Tacker's baby trees were stacked in his garage. He showed them proudly to the visiting scientists. "Ain't been a one of them things down here. I know what's goin' on up north, but I guess they just like the taste of the towns up there."

Parmiter kept slightly behind King as they walked over the barren, frozen soil out to the north pasture where the concrete lay. All of the men wore heavy woolen scarfs and caps, wrapped up to their eyes as a futile defense against the sharp, horizontal wind shrieking across the flat land.

King said, "I don't even see any rocks."

Parmiter replied, "You didn't have to come, Wiley. You could have let us do this."

King shook his head. "Keeps my mind occupied."

They walked along, studying the ground, kicking at small clods of dirt and removing their hands from their pockets only to wipe their eyes, which were streaming from the cold.

They all rested on the concrete slab. Parmiter looked at the other four figures. "Is that Marvin Curtis over there?" Curtis, a well-known zoologist, had just had an article published in *Nature* on sleeping tests of the *parmiteras*.

"Yes. Want to meet him?"

"No," said Parmiter. He kicked at another frigid rock. "They're dead. As far as the South is concerned anyhow. The second generation has just about been used up." Parmiter eyed the concrete slab. "Seems a pity." He stood up, flapping his arms to keep warm. "Well, Wiley, I think I'll head on back to school. You're looking healthy." They chatted for a moment about schools, people, conventions, but it was a short talk because Parmiter had no family to ramble on about.

As King watched Parmiter's thin figure fade toward Tacker's house, one of the Smithsonian people who had flown down to help search for *parmiteras* in the South, walked up to King. "So that's the great James Parmiter."

"He's changed," said King. "Not as dapper as when he danced around my classes."

"Dapper!" The scientist snorted. "He looks like a bloody trash can that hasn't been emptied in years."

It was a relief to get home again. Parmiter hung up his coat and scarf and sat on the sofa trying to decide whether brandy or coffee would wash away the encounters of the past week with Jamis and King. His hand froze just as he was about to pour out some brandy. On the rug were two fresh burns.

Parmiter set the shot glass and bottle back into the cabinet. "Hello," he said happily, knowing the insect heard him, wherever he was in the house.

Clarence was on the table in the dark basement, squatting next to the vivarium as though waiting for Parmiter. Parmiter sprinkled ash into the bowl and asked, "Where's the family, hmm?" He placed the roach into the vivarium. Clarence ate hungrily and ignored Parmiter.

Parmiter heard a tiny ticking sound from behind. His heart pounding, he peered into a corner clogged with cobwebs and dust. He clicked the flashlight on. Instantly there was a rustle of tiny bodies. Then a small brown dot shot out from the molding and paused next to a floor-mounted heating pipe.

Parmiter realized that a dozen roaches were surrounding the pipe, their rust-colored bodies blending in perfectly with the basement. He passed the light over them. They remained motionless. Parmiter noted that in his mind. They were not afraid of light. They were not household bugs.

One of the roaches scooted out of the circle to the center of the floor. Tiny, fragile, and alone, the little creature regarded Parmiter with flickering antennae. Then his legs flashed in complex cadence. The roach glided right up to Parmiter's foot. One sweep of the antennae and the roach climbed upon his shoe. Just as quickly he scurried to the floor again and clambered onto the table leg. He mounted the leg to the top and walked along the edge of the table right up, practically, to Parmiter's face.

He stopped. And Parmiter gently scooped him up. The body was hard but not sealed like Clarence's shell. It had wings, straight and tightly folded, like Madilene's. The antennae were extremely long. The tiny knobbed head had a complete set of eyes. Underneath his tail were two stubby, brittle cerci. A horny patch of flesh in front of them resembled that on Clarence.

Parmiter touched the cerci. A sharp chirp issued forth and Parmiter cursed and dropped the bug, sucking the growing blister on his finger. The roach chirped again as it hit the floor. When Parmiter looked over, he saw the rest of the insects arranged in a semicircle, stampeding directly toward him. Parmiter jumped from the chair, knocking it over. His jaw popped open. Seeing him move apparently confused the roaches. They broke their half circle and milled about in confusion.

They were a colony. No roaches formed colonies. But these were definitely a colony. Parmiter had to get them caged. They could accidentally burn the house down.

The one he had dropped remained on the floor regarding Parmiter with his antennae. He had not moved a bit when Parmiter had jumped. Impossible!

Parmiter pulled on a canvas glove, picked up the bug again, and dropped it into the vivarium with Clarence. Parmiter clapped a wooden board over the vivarium and ran upstairs to get his tape recorder.

He found it at the bottom of a cardboard box full of magazines. He pressed the button to check the batteries, but they were dead as stone and he did not have an AC cord. Parmiter flung the recorder down in disgust and stomped it to pieces.

The chirps of these roaches were different, clear and pure, almost musical, like crickets, as opposed to Clarence's growls. They had come running at that single cry from the one that had burned him. Almost as if they had been called. If Parmiter could record various chirps, he could replay them back to the whole colony. Not just one lonely bug but a nest.

From downstairs chirps worked their way up, piercing through the floors and walls. Parmiter dashed downstairs and found them on the table milling around the vivarium. He counted them. He felt a nervous scurrying from behind him. When he looked back, he jumped violently. Another column of roaches was marching across the floor from beneath the wooden stairs.

Like a snake, the column of bodies wound gracefully up the table legs to the top, where they joined their fellows.

Parmiter counted again. Eighty-two. The milling became more organized and began to slow down. Eventually the roaches stopped, their bodies arranged in a perfect spoked wheel surrounding the vivarium. They remained perfectly still. Patient, watchful. . . .

Parmiter slammed his fist on the table. They did not scatter. They did not move. He put on his glove and picked one up again and dropped it into the bowl, after propping the board against the side of it. The pattern broke and the roaches moved in concert. It happened so suddenly that it seemed as if the circle had exploded, throwing debris around. Parmiter desperately scooped them into his hand to drop them into the bowl.

The chirping began again, clear, piercing, almost ultrasonic. Clarence answered with his lower pitched song. Even Madilene paused at the glass of her tank. Parmiter, eyes bulging, arms out from his side, his senses delivering impossibilities to his brain that struggled to contain them, stepped back and just let them alone.

The roaches were piling into a heap of bodies at the base of the board propped against the bowl. Two of them walked up to the very lip of the vivarium and chirped down at Clarence and the other bug. Both chirped back. Only Madilene in her helmet remained silent. The chirps spread down the board and the bugs trekked up the board to the top of the vivarium and marched right into it, spreading across the earthen piles excitedly, chirping madly all the while, like human passengers boarding a ship for the kind of vacation they hoped will change their lives.

In two days of careful observation, Parmiter gained enough information about the new roaches to fill four full notebook pages.

Rather than ash they ate garbage like any scavenger. Their bodies were not as impervious as Clarence's; a flyswatter could kill one. They showed absolutely no interest in leaving the bowl once they were in it. Every time Parmiter removed a couple and set them on a table, they ran up the board into the vivarium again.

There were three basic types of roach within the colony. The largest, with light-colored heads, were the females; the black medium-sized ones were soldiers; and the smallest of the black ones were workers which moved slower and more reluctantly about the vivarium.

Parmiter saw the sun come up the next morning. He took a sample of each type to school that day. Parmiter sleepwalked through two seminars that morning. Miss Denton, one of his students, handed in another twenty pages and informed him that she would not be around in the summer after all.

When the building emptied at five, Parmiter remained in the lab. He locked the door and dissected all three kinds of insects. They were vulnerable to fire and burned like any insect when set alight.

They had thick, heavy nerve trunks, which meant they could run like hell.

The brains were cricket-shaped with mushroom caps in each hemisphere. Parmiter placed brain tissue onto a slide and focused carefully. The brains were swarming with bacteria. The bead glands now lay at the base of the antennae inside the skull. The glands of the slower bugs were so distended as to impair their nervous systems. They were probably outcasts of a sort or colony morons. The roaches had five eyes, many of which were crowded into blindness by the bacteria.

Was it an accident, Parmiter wondered, that the bacteria had deserted the digestive tract in these creatures or was there a law working here somewhere? The glands strung out into the thorax, but from there on down he might have been examining Madilene. They also had her quinone glands.

In the original *parmitera* the bacteria had served as the most complex and advanced digestive system ever discovered. Parmiter wondered excitedly what kind of a brain they had now.

At home Parmiter carried a spadeful of rich black earth in from his backyard and dropped it into the vivarium. The roaches swarmed over this new interior decoration. Parmiter counted seventy-nine of them exactly. Not one had left the bowl all day.

He saw by their swarming how well attuned to one another they were. They never collided, even in the most frantic of movements. It was then that he realized that two of the females were already pregnant.

It took Max Linden's daughter nearly two hours to drive him into Washington through the clogged traffic of the beltway. She said, "It's not as bad as it was when they didn't have the sound speakers and checked all the cars by hitting them with poles. I never got in till twelve thirty that time." She shifted to neutral and waited for the glacial traffic to unjam itself. "There!" she said. "See it?"

To the side of the road far ahead Linden saw a small booth with L-shaped poles mounted by the road. Traffic was looser on the other side of it. "You drive under and beside those things and it sweeps the car with sound waves and kills the *parmiteras*." They were through and speeding along within minutes. "It's okay so long as you don't have dogs in the car. Ultrasonics drives them batty."

Linden briefly greeted the staff, accepted a welcome-back gift, and walked with his cane to his office. Secretly he was angry at feeling tired after so little exertion. He sat in his chair and propped his cane against the wall. "Have they bred?" he asked an assistant.

"No. And all the females delivered by last week. None have copulated; none are carrying egg cases anymore."

"Call Wiley King, would you?"

After the greetings Linden asked abruptly, "And how is Parmiter?"

"He's become a bit of a hermit. Of course, he always was." A silence. "No one has talked to him for weeks. His assistant is still in the hospital." King described Metbaum's illness. "For instance one day he had a fever of a hundred and ten. Before they could pack him in ice, his fever broke and was back to normal within an hour. His throat swelled up and shrank. It seems that as fast as he has a peculiar relapse, he has a positively *weird* recovery."

"That's all just the bacteria sorting themselves out. They'd never let the host die though. Anything else?"

"Just a few nightmares." King took a deep breath. The plague had hit him personally. "I'm just glad they never bred on the surface. We'd have never been rid of them."

"Lucky us." Linden laughed.

Parmiter was about to dissect another roach when he found himself thinking about something very strange. Rome and Sparta. The silver hammer poised just before chopping the creature in half. He removed the magnifying glass from the head of the *parmitera*. Rome and Sparta. The two ancient cities meant something. Like a combination to a lock he did not know he was confronting till this minute.

Parmiter looked down at the swirling bodies of the roaches, allowing his thoughts to unravel a bit further just to see what would come. Soldiers marching. Leather, armor, and shields. Thermopylae.

Arrow battles. The great armies of the ancient world. The egg case. Rome and Sparta had something to do with the egg case.

The colony lined up along the edge of the table watching Parmiter. Parmiter said, "I don't suppose Rome and Sparta mean anything to you. I don't suppose anything I do means anything to you."

He went into the kitchen to prepare some breadcrumbs and water for them. When he returned, the insects had aligned their bodies with the handwriting on some of his checks scattered on the table. Parmiter sternly shook them off the papers. They slowly wound their way up the sides of the glass into the bowl.

Parmiter sat in his office till he heard the high heel clack of one of his students. Denise Denton was the only girl he had ever met who was truly unintimidated by insects crawling up her arms. She sat down on the chair opposite his desk. She smiled at him. She was both flattered and curious. "Here I am," she told him cheerfully.

"Miss Denton. I'm glad you closed the door. Ready?"

"I think so."

"I'll precede with a lecture. You realize that scientists work the same way artists do, the same way. They sense truth by the aesthetics of a theory rather than by dead facts. There's something aesthetic in back of my head about the *parmiteras* and I can't nail it down. I thought I'd try a free association test with you."

"On the roaches."

"Are you game?"

She wiped a lock of brown hair back from her oval face and squeezed her eyes shut. "I've done this myself. Roaches . . . roaches . . . Okay. Go ahead."

"Two words."

Eyes still shut, she repeated, "Two words."

"Rome and Sparta."

Miss Denton frowned a bit. She immediately said, "Greek and Latin. Or rather the other way round."

"Do you feel as silly as I do?"

"Rome and Sparta were city states. They both were at war.

Sparta consisted of the most stoic, relentless, and cruel of soldiers. A masculine, rigid society. Rome had the Roman legions. . . ." As Parmiter took notes, she opened her eyes. "Maybe that's something. Both were very warlike."

"Rome and Sparta. And roaches."

She mumbled, "Empires . . . relentless . . . fighting . . . weaponry. I'm sorry, all it means is a kind of relentlessness to me. Isn't that strange? Roaches are survivors, living fossils. Maybe it's in there somewhere."

Parmiter put down his clipboard. "That will do, thank you. It's been driving me a bit crazy." He rustled through a stack of papers till he found her thesis. "I looked through this, Miss Denton. I didn't know you'd been at the Anti-Locust Center in London."

"Oh yes. I met a man who worked with Faure when he postulated locustine. I hope to go back this summer. May I ask how Metbaum is, Doctor Parmiter?"

"Progressing."

"We miss him."

Parmiter wondered if they would miss him if he had been bitten and hospitalized. Then he decided he did not care. "Locustine is the second reason I wanted to speak to you. You claim it's an explanation of how acquired traits can be passed onto the young."

"That's right."

"Most of evolutionary biology would land on you for that. Kammerer committed suicide over it." Paul Kammerer, the last major scientist to question whether—as many sneered—a mother who lost her tail would give birth to tailless offspring, died as a victim of total vilification from his colleagues.

Miss Denton said, "Faure theorized that locustine was a substance consisting of waste products. The stuff collects in the blood vessel walls and tissues of the regular grasshopper, making it restless and driving it to cluster with others. When grasshoppers aggregate in groups larger than what they're accustomed to, they begin to resemble locusts. Their colors become darker; they get bigger. . . ."

"Why do they cluster in the first place?"

"Nobody knows, Dr. Parmiter. Barometric changes. Temperature. Food. They just do sometimes. Anyway these waste products, this locustine, is transferred from the body of the mother through the blood to the yolks of her eggs, leaving the offspring with an abnormally high concentration of it at birth. The infants are born frenzied and highly active; they aggregate into even tighter groups, lay more eggs, and the cycle continues until they're breeding in the millions. Then you get a cloud of locusts."

"Anything that cannot discharge waste products poisons itself," Parmiter objected. "Any larvae born with it is poisoned at birth. . . ."

"That's the point! Locusts are abnormalities! The grasshopper in the state of migration is not a stable species."

"Thank you, Miss Denton. I'll remember you to Metbaum when I see him."

Parmiter wrote it out neatly. The locustine theory described what Clarence had done with the bacteria. He had transferred it by saliva to the eggs. When the offspring had hatched, they were as different from their parents as locusts were from simple grasshoppers.

Parmiter brought home a cardboard carton containing a maze and an electric cage to experiment with the bugs. He set the box on the basement table and counted the roaches. One of them was missing. He searched all through the house but did not find it. At one thirty he went to the hospital to visit Metbaum.

Metbaum had had a relapse. One of the bacteria strains had burst forth in virulent delayed strength, making him feverish but energetic. He looked up at Parmiter from his bed with eyes that glittered. "God sent the *parmiteras* to teach man fire back in prehistory, Doc."

Parmiter sat down hesitantly, wondering whether to call a nurse or not. "Really?" he asked.

"Yeah. God, man was intelligent as far back as fifty thousand years. They can tell from moon phase markings on mastodon bones." Metbaum jabbed a finger at Parmiter for emphasis. "Right? Goddamn right. Goddamn," Metbaum muttered as his eyes closed.

Parmiter was intrigued by the theory. The cockroach had surely been the most common animal in prehistory, and one theory had it that forest fires had been the major cause of man's line of development. Fires had driven the tree-dwelling apeman into the grasslands, where his intelligence and instincts were sharpened by the ground-based predators stalking there. When man had ceased to be a tree dweller, he had become a human. Suppose the *parmiteras* had caused the great forest fires back then. Suppose man had watched the rubbing cerci, then had looked at two twigs. . . .

Parmiter said, "Very good, Metbaum. You are aware, I suppose, that *Australopithecus Africanus* was the earliest user of tools. Your theory would presuppose that there was a trace of *parmitera* in southern Africa. . . ."

Metbaum heard nothing. He muttered and murmured in fever.

When the nurse came in, she saw the entomologist talking loudly to the feverish patient as though a class of students were facing him. "Sir?" she asked.

Parmiter froze, and he looked back at her with a trace of fear in his eyes at what he had been doing.

The instant he walked in his door again, Parmiter felt that prickle at the back of his neck that reassured him that he knew exactly what the bugs were up to. The missing *parmitera* was on the coffee table observing him.

Parmiter searched his den for an old paint set he had once bought for touching up lamps and bric-a-brac. He found the set and a stiff brush at the bottom of a cabinet.

He picked up the waiting *parmitera* and daubed a swatch of brass-colored paint on the creature's back. The roach nestled snugly in his hand. In the basement none of the other insects stirred when Parmiter dropped Goldback into the vivarium. "Goldback," he said, "we know each other now."

Parmiter went in to pour a glass of milk for lunch. As he carried the glass into the living room, Parmiter heard a chirp from the windowsill. It was Goldback again. He had rushed back upstairs. Apparently he had been chosen to shadow Parmiter. Several others were out of the bowl, huddling on the basement table around pieces of paper covered with Parmiter's doodling. "Get in the bowl. Come on, come on," he said, dropping them back in. Placing a good heavy board over the bowl, Parmiter carried it upstairs into the kitchen. He unpacked the maze and the cage and prepared for two experiments. Goldback scurried in behind him and remained in a corner watching him.

Parmiter's maze and cage experiments were duplicates of the experiments performed by C. H. Turner in 1912. Turner had been one of the greatest black biologists, one of the very few human beings, besides Parmiter, who liked the company of roaches.

Parmiter's wire cage was the size of a shoebox and was divided in two by a wood partition. Half of it was wrapped in foil to close out light. The two halves were connected by a small opening in the wood partition, and a copper wire strip, connected to batteries, lined this opening. Into the darkened compartment Parmiter placed a dab of mayonnaise mixed with sugar.

Parmiter's maze was constructed of metal strips meandering through plywood walls. In the center was the mayonnaise and sugar. Parmiter placed both devices next to each other on his kitchen table. He was going to conduct both experiments simultaneously, a violation of standard practice, but Parmiter was impatient to get moving.

The electric cage was designed to implant reflexes in insects. Normally a roach heads for the dark, where there is food and shelter. Upon passing the electrified strip, however, the roach gets a shock and learns to avoid darkness, thus overcoming one of its basic instincts. Although the *parmiteras* did not react to light, they would go for the food. By pulling them out of the cage for certain lengths of time, then putting them back in for another run, Parmiter could learn how retentive their memories were.

After trying to decide whether a female or a soldier would make the best subject, Parmiter decided on Goldback. He gently picked him off the floor, whispering, "Easy, little fellow, easy. Don't be afraid." He placed him in the beginning of the maze run and locked him there in a small compartment. From the vivarium Parmiter withdrew a worker and locked him inside the electric cage. He tested the electricity. He set his stopwatch on the table. Then he released both bugs into their own obstacle courses and watched them.

The watch ticked. Goldback blundered along a plywood passage. The worker headed immediately for the electric strip. It paused nervously at the threshold and poked its long antennae into the darkened compartment. Then one foreleg touched the copper strip. The roach gave a loud chirp and leaped backwards. In the maze, Goldback froze at the sound of the chirp. His antennae searched the air. Again the worker stepped up to the copper plate. It waited for an instant. Then it put one foreleg on the electric trap and kept it there.

A sweet smell of quinones drifted upward from the worker. The foreleg shivered at the current, then poked forward into the compartment. Incredible!

Then Parmiter noticed the vivarium. The entire colony was lined up on the lip of the bowl, antennae pointed like gun barrels toward him. The stopwatch read one hundred and seventeen seconds. The worker gingerly put three legs onto the copper strip. Then with a rush he vanished into the darkened half of the cage. And chirped.

At the second chirp, Goldback resumed his exploration of the maze. After an elapsed time of one hundred and twenty-eight seconds, he was in the center contentedly chewing on the mayonnaise.

Parmiter put the worker back into the vivarium and watched the others surround it like a family greeting the prodigal son. He carefully lifted two soldiers from the squirming bodies and put them into the electric cage. Parmiter did not even have time to turn on his stopwatch. Both soldiers raced fearlessly over the copper strip into the dark compartment as if electricity did not exist. Parmiter checked the batteries. Perfectly charged.

He fixed some coffee laced with brandy and doodled on a sketch pad. The electric cage created Pavlovian reflexes. It replaced the instinct to go after food with an instinct to avoid food by associating food with pain.

Yet these bugs just learned to overcome pain. New reflexes gained by applied agony did not appear. It could be weakened survival instincts or overwhelming hunger drives. Something strong enough to hold pain reflexes in abeyance. It could be another instinct or instincts that made the roach test the electricity rather than run from it. Just like a human. What kind of instinct was subtle enough to do that? Curiosity? Just like in humans.

Parmiter doodled and let the thoughts come. Something to do with the bacteria. And strong enough to be communicated rapidly to the others. No danger, said the instinct. After thirty minutes Parmiter wrote on the pad, "Time Elapsed—thirty minutes."

Parmiter replaced Goldback with a soldier who took one hundred and seventy seconds to get through the maze. Then, after another ten minutes, Parmiter put Goldback in again to see how well he remembered the maze. This time Goldback ran through in forty-two seconds. *Forty-two seconds!*

It was not a perfect run. Goldback bumped against a wall, paused, and continued to the end. Parmiter placed Goldback in the electric cage. Goldback tangled antennae with his fellows for an instant, then unhesitantly crossed the electric threshold.

Parmiter rapidly made some more notes. Hunger instincts were hard to block. The roaches did not respond to Pavlovian experiments. The memories of the bugs were extremely retentive. And. . . .

Parmiter set the notepaper on the table. From the electric cage he removed the first worker he had put in, the one who originally tested the electricity. The worker was placed in the maze. He ran it in fifty seconds flat. Except for one error. He bumped into the same piece of maze as Goldback.

Parmiter took a female out of the aquarium and put her into the maze. Forty-four seconds. He tried a soldier. Forty seconds. And every one of them made Goldback's wrong turn.

Parmiter examined his notes. Then he tore them up and stuffed them into the wastebasket. Nobody would believe this. He dumped the entire colony into the electric cage. They crawled and ran and cavorted over the electricity as though it were a mild draft.

When he returned them to the basement, he found Madilene forlornly rooting through the now-dusty pressure tank. He took her upstairs and ran her through the maze. It took her five minutes. She sprayed Parmiter's fingers with quinones every time he prodded her to keep her from falling asleep. Once she tried to eat the walls; once she tried climbing out. When she got to the center she eagerly consumed every speck of mayonnaise and searched for more.

Parmiter had found out what he had wanted to know about the *parmiteras*. They communicated with one another. Almost instantaneously. They communicated so well that they could describe mazes and wrong turns. And they could alert others to danger. Clever. Very clever. Compared to Madilene who now hissed stupidly at him. . . .

Winter gripped the Eastern Seaboard. Record snowfalls buried New England. In the cities of the north a power crisis, caused by strict rationing of fossil fuel burning and subsequent smoking of the air, grew to where the death toll from pneumonia and respiratory diseases caused a run on medicines, whose prices were jacked up with the explanation that shortages were critical.

In late January the New Jersey State Highway Commission reported that they had not found a *parmitera*-infested car for two days over the entire state. The highway patrols of Maryland and Virginia reported that cars had been clean for nearly a week. The Department of Agriculture backed up by Linden in the Smithsonian and the Museum of Natural History expressed cautious hope. The plague was breaking. The constant rain and snow had dampened inflammable structures. It looked as if the roaches were not equipped to survive winter.

By now it had become obvious to Parmiter that the roaches found him as interesting as he found them. They climbed out of the bowl and lost themselves in the ever more unwieldy pile of papers growing on his basement table. All twenty-eight of the females were pregnant and carrying egg cases in a small pouch of their abdomens close to the vulva.

Parmiter spoke to Goldback whenever he saw him. "Look out there!" he said, as he stepped over the bug or "Get out of that window there or you'll freeze to death."

One day Parmiter decided to move them out of the basement and up to his den. So he cleared off his desk for them and put down a clean green blotter while moving the soft white fluorescent lamp so that it would shine straight down into the vivarium. He set the glass bowl on the blotter and wired it shut. Then he drew the curtains.

That night Parmiter's nightmares came back to him. He heard the chirp just as he lay down in bed. He thought it was a random sound from the vivarium until he found himself facing an opening, corrugated mouth that split and laterally parted into a dozen pieces like a jigsaw puzzle. When the mouth closed, the pieces miraculously fitted together again with an ease that belied their complexity. The parts separated again, yawning wide in a strange forced way, and Parmiter was awake. At first he thought it had happened because he was subconsciously unused to sleeping in his own bedroom. Nevertheless, something was happening with the roaches. The instant he sat up in bed, several of them stopped chirping.

Rome and Sparta! It hit him! The children! The Spartans had thrown their weakest infants onto hillsides to die of exposure. And in latter-day Rome the upper classes had considered it unfashionable to have children, so they practiced infanticide. No one knew on how large a scale this was done, but it had happened.

Parmiter heard the singing of the crickets outside, bravely piping above the ocean of his backyard. Lost and lonely those sounds, those sad strange singings of unearthly lives.

Rome and Sparta. Parmiter dug his fists into his temples. He did not have it all yet, not quite all of it. The idea was like a submerged log that bobbed tantalizingly to sight then sank every time he reached for it. Parmiter switched on the light.

Goldback stood at the door-molding. The others were in the vivarium. Parmiter said out loud, "It's something to do with children, with offspring. I know my own life. What I'm thinking now is something to do with science, some law that explains certain kinds of misery. . . ."

They began chirping. The chirping built, gathered, timed its pulses to his words, then died away with his silence. He discovered the roaches on a painting on the wall as he came into the room. "Come on down, come on, damn it!" The bugs remained there until Parmiter shook the picture. They swarmed down the wall and stopped at the bottom molding just short of the floor.

"Well, come on," he repeated. Then Parmiter saw it. He stooped down until he was eye level with them, looked up at the picture, then back at the insects. A cold sheet softly covered his spine. The painting they had vacated was a still life of summer sunlight pouring through an open window. The pattern the roaches made was the exact outline of the painted window.

Parmiter gathered them up and put them into the vivarium. He sat at his desk and shakily drew a huge sketch of a right triangle on a piece of manila paper. He scooped some of the bugs out of the bowl and shook them onto the paper. They hugged the outline of the triangle.

Parmiter carried the paper with the roaches still clinging to it over to the wall. He shook the paper violently and the roaches scurried off the paper and onto the wall where they re-formed themselves into a triangle.

Parmiter drew swirls and stars and blossoms, and wavy lines on paper. The roaches kept up the game and duplicated all the drawings on the wall, no matter how complex. Parmiter tried different colored inks. The roaches still made patterns. None of the paper had a trace of quinones after they had left. None of the ink had been eaten.

Before the afternoon was over, the roaches took the initiative. They rooted through his papers onto the sheets of doodles Parmiter made, and formed their bodies along the crazed, jagged drawings. Parmiter saw no sense to it, no attraction the patterns could have. Unlike the sexual or aggressive responses of certain butterflies and fishes to body markings, the *parmiteras'* interest in patterns seemed to be chaotic. They were interested in Parmiter's writing. That was the only sense he could see.

He called the grocery store to have his weekly allotment of food delivered. Parmiter did not have to read from a list. He had been ordering the same items each week for a couple of months. "Four roast beef TV dinners. Four cans of mushroom soup. Five quarts of milk. Four quarts of orange juice and a can of coffee."

The clerk said, "Sorry, Mr. Parmiter, I didn't hear that last one. There's something wrong with the line."

"I beg your pardon?"

"There's some kind of screaming on this line. Hear it?"

"No . . . I . . ." Parmiter heard it then. But it was not on the phone; it was from his house. The roaches were chirping. It had begun so low and built up to a crescendo so gradually that Parmiter had been unaware of it.

Goldback came into the room, and Parmiter watched his minute, arrogant progress across the rug to the coffee table.

Parmiter said, "That last was a can of coffee. You know my brand."

"What?" asked the clerk.

The chirping that had drowned out Parmiter's words stopped.

"Coffee! My brand. And leave it on the doorstep; don't come into the house."

Parmiter slammed down the phone and pulled out the plug. He looked at Goldback. The chirping had stopped altogether. It would not start again unless Parmiter spoke. He saw the method to it. The roaches had chirped in time to his words. They were trying to mimic him.

It was a standard hydrocarbon-based insecticide that Parmiter had picked up in a supermarket. He found it in the back of a kitchen cabinet. Parmiter tightly wired the vivarium shut, then threw two blankets over it. He did not want the other roaches to hear Goldback.

Goldback allowed himself to be carried into the kitchen. He regarded Parmiter as the entomologist closed the doors to the study and the kitchen, then approached with the spray can held out.

Parmiter's heart thumped wildly. But he had no choice; he had to know if they were invulnerable, like Clarence, or as sensitive to poison as Madilene. He held the spray can about ten inches from Goldback and pressed the valve. Two seconds of spray floated out and settled gently over the insect. Parmiter looked at his watch and counted. Goldback became rigid, then unfroze and backed nervously toward the wall of the sink. He was halfway up when the trembling began. The legs scratched madly for a foothold, then the bug slid back down into the sink. Goldback walked in a circle twice, his pace becoming increasingly ragged, for his legs were uncontrollably vibrating like plucked harp strings.

Twenty seconds. Parmiter felt the sweat pour down his face. Suddenly Goldback began shrieking at a volume tremendous enough to well into the air like an expanding ball. It was a clear pulsating scream of agony compressed into a hollow, ringing tone by the sink walls. Parmiter clapped his hands to his ears. God, the others would hear it; nothing could contain that noise!

Goldback shrieked for some ten seconds before the muscle controlling the cerci began failing, breaking the chirp up into grating, uneven bursts that lowered steadily in intensity, becoming weaker and more uncertain, and finally stopping altogether. Goldback then flipped onto his back, legs digging madly at the air. Then even that stopped. The legs curled tightly against the body which bent painfully as Goldback struggled for air. The body slowly relaxed. Parmiter knew Goldback was dead. Seventy-eight seconds.

From the den came the combined banshee shrieks of the other *parmiteras,* mounting higher and higher, pouring through the stuffing over the vivarium, through the walls and doors, a chorus of primitive rage and blind hate at the world containing them.

Parmiter's hand was trembling. He mopped his face. Holding the spray can before him like a lance, he opened the door and slowly made his way into the den.

It was going to be a beautiful Saturday. Last night's snowfall had coated the campus in blinding white. Students were having snowball fights in the quadrangle.

Parmiter finished his milk in the cafeteria and hurried as fast as he could over the ice-clad walks for home. Near the parking lot next to Carson Hall, he heard his name called out. He looked back at the figure bundled up in the overcoat with a flapping scarf up to the eyes. Metbaum. Parmiter looked him up and down. "When did you get out, Metbaum?"

"Two days ago. I tried to get you in your office." Metbaum's cheeks were thin but flushed. He was still underweight, but he did not look so tired.

"How are you feeling then?"

"It should happen to everybody. I'm gaining my weight back. They all think I'll live to a hundred and fifty. I'm immune to vaccination and probable infection. Wait till I start eating ashes. I'm going to knock off for a semester and relax."

"Good, Metbaum. Good idea."

Metbaum looked curiously up at one of the speakers. "So that's what did it."

"So far. There hasn't been a new fire blamed on them in two weeks. It's interesting if you walk around. You see their shells everywhere. They decay very slowly. . . ."

"You ought to give that Linden a call sometime. Tell him about the pressure tank. . . . What's wrong?"

Parmiter's face had blanched. "Metbaum, I hope you didn't tell him anything!"

"I haven't talked to him. Don't look so worried—it was just a suggestion."

After that, they could think of nothing much to say. Metbaum finally said, "How about a cup of coffee?"

"Afraid I have to get home, Metbaum."

"Oh."

They walked for a moment. Then Metbaum stuck his hand out. "This is where I leave. Don't forget to write, Doc."

As Metbaum walked away, Parmiter felt a growing frustration. He wanted to say something more friendly but did not know how. "Will you be back, Metbaum?"

"Next September."

Parmiter watched Metbaum's thin figure walk across the white snow until it was gone. He felt something break loose within him, like a mooring that had broken, releasing a craft which he had been riding all along without realizing it.

Home. He plugged in the phone and called the Smithsonian and asked for Max Linden. "This is James Parmiter, Dr. Linden."

A stunned silence. "Parmiter. So you do exist after all."

"Yes." He laughed. "There's been something I've been meaning to ask."

"There's a lot we wanted to ask you, James. But go ahead."

"After we found out about the pressure, did anyone ever try to breed the *parmiteras?*"

"Why yes. They did it up at the Museum of Natural History. They succeeded too. I believe it was in some device they use for. . . ."

"What happened to the infants?"

"They were all left in the tank for several days. The infants were blind. They didn't grow as fast as the surface ones did; in fact, I expect their metabolisms are the same as in other species. Did you try to breed them?"

As both men talked, Parmiter's roaches filed slowly up the wall. They arranged themselves on a blank space next to a seascape painting. Their bodies moved around briefly and became still, forming the two words—JAMES PARMITER.

"Yes. But nothing ever came of it. What happened after all that?" Parmiter kept his eyes on the roaches.

"They were destroyed of course. Wouldn't do to have another plague. Well, tell me about yourself, Parmiter!"

At last Parmiter hung up the phone. He unplugged it again. He was undisturbed in the house.

JAMES PARMITER.

He closed and locked all the doors and windows, then he brought the vivarium into the living room. He sat on the sofa and said clearly, "Three plus two."

Their bodies spelled it out. 5.

Parmiter said, "Remember what I told you yesterday. One chirp for yes. Two chirps for no. Do you understand?"

They answered with one chirp.

Parmiter smiled.

Goldback's murder had been the watershed. Trauma probably. The big God on two feet had taken one of them away. The sound and sight of Parmiter did not mean as much to the bugs as whatever mysterious vibrations their antennae picked up. So it was not surprising that they had no trouble traversing from the sight of the written word to the sound of the spoken word. And they had gained a rudimentary vocabulary from Parmiter's habit of talking to himself and them.

It could have been anything. The spark, the little trigger that had actually made them think, was as mysterious in them as it was in humans. The fact that they were a colony had something to do with it. But of all the incredibility of the event, the strangest thing was Parmiter's own reaction to it. He was a trifle disappointed. It was something like the giant squid, which had been far more frightening as a fearsome legend than as an actual fact once it had been discovered to exist.

Parmiter had shaken the earth from his dingy basement in a lost college town. He had communicated with another species. And in four days it was already old hat to him.

"X," said Parmiter.

X.

"7 and 4," he said.

7. Then 4.

"No, no. Add them."

11.

"Bowl."

The roaches climbed down the wall and filed back into the vivarium.

Parmiter rested his chin in his hand and contemplated them. They had memories that were superb. They could remember the associations between words and actions, commands and movements.

He thought over every idea he could conjure up to explain his success. In the end Parmiter gave up and just stared sightlessly, thoughtlessly, wonderingly, and proudly at the forest of antennae waving at him behind the thick glass.

They left the bowl quietly that evening. It was the first time they had done so drastic an act since Parmiter had communicated with them. He found them on the floor of the den. For some reason they were tormenting Clarence, climbing over his waddling shell and tearing at his legs.

Parmiter said, "Listen!" There came a weak chirp from one roach. They continued ripping at the aged bug. Parmiter stamped his foot. "Wall! Wall!"

The roaches broke up and swarmed up the wall on command. Five females remained on the floor with Clarence. They savagely badgered the huge bug as he desperately turned in a circle to escape their mandibles and antennae, their probing and clicking and tangling of legs.

"Listen to me," cried Parmiter.

One chirp.

"What the hell are you doing?"

A word formed from their floating bodies: GO.

"Why?"

GO.

"I will not! I live in this house!"

NO.

The pregnant females stood a distance off from the bulk of the colony. As Parmiter watched, Clarence finally began getting angry. He kicked feebly at one of the soldiers and buzzed menacingly.

Parmiter thought he understood. They considered Clarence an entirely different species and therefore a potential threat to the females. But it was an extraordinarily aggressive defense. They had to pile into his tank and drag him all the way out to kill him. These soldiers and workers guarded the females as bees guarded pregnant queens. They took reproduction very seriously, even more than survival. And these eggs were almost ready to hatch.

The murder of Goldback had traumatized them in more ways than one. They had become so dependent on or awestruck with Parmiter that they were delaying their migration with the eggs until the last possible moment. Parmiter's sense of their life rhythm was so far accurate. He had sensed how strong their bonds to him were and so allowed them to run about the house. Now the growing pressure of hatching was interfering with this dependence. They were disregarding Parmiter to an alarming degree.

"Listen," said Parmiter.

One chirp.

"Wall!" said Parmiter.

Reluctantly they left Clarence and began climbing the wall and spreading out.

"Stay!" said Parmiter.

He reached down for one of the pregnant females on the rug.

Two chirps. Instantly they were pouring back onto the floor.

"Stay!" bellowed Parmiter. His hand poised in the air over the female.

Two chirps.

"Yes!" cried Parmiter.

Silence.

Parmiter turned instead to Clarence. He carefully brushed away the females surrounding him and lifted him. One of the females had Clarence's leg in her mandibles. She rose up as Parmiter lifted Clarence and hung on tightly.

Two chirps. Two chirps. Two chirps.

"Let go, damn you, let go!"

Two chirps. Two chirps. Two chirps.

Parmiter gently touched the female with his forefinger.

Two chirps. Two chirps. Two chirps.

Suddenly there were only two roaches on the wall. The rest of the colony was on the rug, rapidly spreading out like an opening fan until Parmiter was enclosed in a half circle that divided the living room.

There was a breathless instant of silence. Then the entire colony unleashed in banshee cries a wailing screech of sawing cerci that ignited a dull orange spark on the wool rug beneath each body. The scorch marks raced outward, joined each other, and flickered into little spurts of flame. In an instant the room had filled with acrid smoke.

Don't panic, don't panic! Parmiter carried Clarence into the study. Just before he dropped the ancient bug into the tank, it began chirping in time with the others, a belated response to whatever they called forth in his own memory.

Parmiter felt a hot branding iron touch his hand. He cursed and threw Clarence into the tank, then rushed back into the living room.

"Stop!" he roared. Instantly the chirping ceased.

The rug sizzled and sputtered. At least it wouldn't burn down the house.

"Wall, you bastards! *Wall!*"

The roaches climbed the wall.

"Stay!" Parmiter cried. His eyes stung with tears and he coughed from the smoke. He ran into the kitchen and returned carrying the insecticide and a small plastic bucket filled with water, which he emptied onto the rug. Clouds of stinking smoke hissed and bellied against the ceiling.

Parmiter slid the vivarium across the floor with his foot. "Listen!"

One chirp.

"Bowl!"

One chirp.

They filed in obediently. Even the females.

Parmiter wired two heavy sheets of screen over the top of the vivarium.

Ernest Jamis, Bainboro's director of development, was up at three in the morning, worrying, smoking, and sipping port. His wife was asleep in the bedroom. Her peaceful breathing was a contrast to the sounds of a sleeping house. She was alive; the rest were just elements—wood walls meeting at floor and ceiling joints all within an ocean of air. Such was life.

Jamis was flying off to Minneapolis the next day to talk to a very important man in trucking. He was going to ask him to contribute money for construction of a new dormitory which would very likely be named after him. Jamis usually had a pitch ready in his mind by this time. However, he had other things worrying him. His secretary Janine was mad at him. She felt used. She had cried a lot this afternoon after he had closed the door to his office.

Jamis stoked the fire in the hearth, being careful not to get his new robe dirty. He had started at Bainboro in order to work his way to where he could land a better position at a big university. But he had read last week that statistics showed that after a certain age academic people tend to stay right where they are for the rest of their lives. Jamis had flung the magazine into the trash can. He was at the age they mentioned and the trouble was he just could not organize himself these days. He was taking things too easy.

The phone rang. The sound exploded the silence into darting pieces that retreated into corners untouched by the lamplight.

"Yes," barked Jamis.

It was Doctor Parmiter. He was very curt. "Come to my house right away, Jamis. The females have all disappeared."

Jamis laughed inadvertently. "Maybe they didn't like your technique."

"Come over here, Jamis. Quickly."

"What *are* you talking about?"

"*Parmiteras*. They will all disappear during gestation. It's beginning now and I have to show them to somebody."

"Wall!" said Parmiter. And they scurried up to the wall, finding a blank part so their shape could more easily be seen.

Jamis looked uneasily down at the burned rug. The man was cracking up; he lived in a filth hole reeking with discarded newspapers.

Parmiter's den smelled unbelievable—an unearthly concentrated mixture of perspiration and sour food. Parmiter, he thought, must live in this room. All the windows were shut, closing off all hope of ventilation. Jamis now knew why Parmiter wanted him over here.

Parmiter had talked so rapidly and drunkenly that Jamis had become aware only too late of the square bowl half full of earth with the shiny dark shapes nestled within. And to his ultimate horror Parmiter had let them loose. The horror was not imagined. The bowl was full of insects.

Their swarming up the wall nearly made Jamis faint. He had entomophobia: fear of insects. Every detail of the night was burned upon his mind, magnified into looming legs of insects reaching out to grasp and scratch at him.

"Parmiter!" roared Jamis. "Stop it!"

"Listen!" cried Parmiter. He grabbed Jamis' sleeve as he tried to stumble out the door.

One single livid chirp. Jamis went white.

"Watch them, Ernest, watch them!" Parmiter forced Jamis to look at the wall. He yelled at the roaches "Parmiter! Show it!" He slowly forced Jamis around to face the wall.

PARMITER.

"Jesus," whispered Jamis. His eyes fought against the sight, but they kept looking anyway, scanning the pattern, looking for tricks, wires, anything.

PARMITER.

"It's a trick!" he said.

Parmiter said to them, "Do you understand me? Spell it out."

The myriad bodies broke up the name, blended and rushed around the wall then stopped.

YES.

"Parmiter, what the hell are they?"

"They're *parmiteras*. Second generation. I bred them with a *Gromphadorhina*."

"Get them off the wall, for God's sake, Parmiter! They'll be all over the place!"

"No, they won't. There are exactly seventy-eight. Fifty actually. The twenty-eight females are gone. These are soldiers and workers."

"Parmiter, you're *crazy!* You belong in a jail! The goddamned nerve of you letting these things loose. . . ."

"They won't leave me yet, Ernest. And they'll be right back after they do."

"Shut up, shut up, shut up! You stupid bastard, you're crazy, Parmiter, crazy! A man doesn't keep these things in a home!"

"I *had* to! I had to stay close to them! Do you think I could have ever gotten them to do this in a lab?"

Awe slowly displaced the rage in Jamis as the import of what he was beholding sunk in. He could not look away from the wall.

"You liar! You son of a bitch, Parmiter, why didn't you tell anybody! These things are dangerous!"

"Ernest, I am part of their life; they could no more imagine being away from me for long than you could stop breathing oxygen for long."

"You said there were some missing already! How many?"

Parmiter nodded at the wall, his mouth stretched in a small, tight smile. "Ask them. Go on, they won't bite you."

Jamis looked at the wall. He opened his mouth and closed it again. "I can't. No, I refuse, Parmiter."

Parmiter said in loud measured tones, "How many of you are missing?"

28.

"Where are the females?"

GONE.

"Gone where?"

GONE.

"Will they all come back?"

YES.

"With the young?"

YES.

"That settles that. Roaches don't lie, I don't think."

Jamis looked carefully on the torn stuffed chair in front of the desk before he sat in it. "How did you do this, Parmiter?"

"They did it mostly. The nearest I can guess is that that bacteria can duplicate even the neural centers and nerve fibers of a brain. Given their numbers and given the fact that nerve cells throughout the animal world are similar, they may have just duplicated the clusters of ganglia within the roaches' bodies. Only that's a quantum step short of intelligence. I don't know if they are really intelligent. Symbols they understand by my wandering around the house talking to myself. And writing. But there's no doubt in your mind, I hope, that I am literally speaking to them and they are answering."

"No doubt," said Jamis, looking up at Parmiter. He gazed hard and thoughtfully at the bony features of the entomologist. "Can they make fire?"

"Yeah. They're regular flamethrowers."

"Jesus!" muttered Jamis, hitting the table in disgust. "Parmiter, I don't care if you go to bed with them. They are *dangerous!* Don't you understand that?"

"Are you *stupid,* Jamis? Don't your gray cells absorb the information I have been giving you so carefully?" Red flecks sparked in Parmiter's eyes. "You *will* listen to me, Jamis!"

Jamis' law training made him suddenly realize how all that he had just seen converged. Parmiter's glaring. The condition of the room. Parmiter's nervousness. He became very still. His voice became calm. He was calculating now. "I apologize, James. May I call you James?"

Parmiter was mollified. "Very well."

"It's too big to get used to quickly. May I ask you some things?"

"Of course."

"You have kept all this very secretive. Why?"

"It's no secret. I'm telling you, aren't I?"

"That's not the real reason, James. Tell me the real reason. Please?"

Parmiter blinked. And thought. And looked at the bugs with a small gesture of helplessness. "Because they're mine, I suppose. I did it all alone. I'm proud of it, and I want sole credit for it. Is that wrong?"

"Didn't Metbaum help?"

"There! That's exactly it, Jamis! A little credit here, a little there, Linden and his crowd gets in on it. . . ."

Jamis looked at the wall also. "James, listen, please. They are running loose. . . ."

"They won't leave me."

"James, please. They also cannot travel, right? Remember that mistake? At a cost of billions of dollars and thousands of deaths, we have rid this country of these things and you've gone and bred some others. Why didn't you do it in a *lab?* Okay, they're yours! It's a hell of an achievement, James. But"—Jamis waved at the trash on the floor and the dirt—"why like *this?*"

"How can I make them trust me, work for me, under a goddamned microscope, Jamis! You don't raise children like that!" Parmiter turned and yelled at the roaches. "Are you all going to leave me?"

YES.

"But you'll be back, won't you?"

YES.

"This man here is named Jamis. Spell his name."

JAMIS.

Jamis looked at the half-resentful, half-proud smile on Parmiter's face. Now he understood why he had been called to this haven of solitude to witness Parmiter's private wonders. Reality had caught up to the strain of too much loneliness. Parmiter neither wanted nor was able to conceal the insects much longer. He had to tell somebody whose opinion he respected before the bugs were all over town, and for some reason he had picked Jamis as a worthy audience.

Parmiter continued talking to the director of development with the same detached, lecturing tone of the schoolmaster. "I worked at it, too, after Goldback died. Alphabet cards. Numbers. They only had to look at a thing once to duplicate it. And as this information grew and I continued talking around the house, the connections were made."

Jamis was slumped forward in his chair, his head in his hands. Parmiter smiled with satisfaction.

Finally Jamis looked up at Parmiter. His eyes were unnaturally alert, his whole body tense and nervous as an animal in a trap waiting for something to happen. His voice was hoarse. "Parmiter, I am going to make you an offer. Are you listening?"

"I'm listening."

"Either you get those horrors into that bowl and into the biology lab tomorrow and you call up Linden or you get some other qualified people to examine them and you do this fast or else. . . ."

"Or else what?"

Jamis stood up. He stood very close to Parmiter talking directly into his face. "Or else you kill them."

Parmiter returned the stare.

Neither man noticed the wall. Silently the bugs formed one word three times.

NO. NO. NO.

"Why?"

"Parmiter, if they can make fire we will have another plague. Now I'm no biologist or anybody's idea of an animal lover, but I know that even with nice little dogs, regardless of how you cut it, *you can't ultimately trust an animal's instincts!* That is a *fact* that every biologist will tell you. *You cannot trust animals!* The tamest dog will bite; the most peaceful cat will accidentally claw a child. And these are insects, damn it. You don't even know what kind of instincts they have!"

"Ernest, these are more intelligent than any animal alive," Parmiter replied patiently.

"Parmiter, man is intelligent and you can't trust *his* instincts! I sure as hell cannot trust *yours!* Intelligence cannot save or change the behavior of *anything*. Get them to the school tomorrow, Parmiter."

"I'll resign!"

Jamis was on his way out the door. "Go ahead. But whatever happens, people are going to have to know about this. If you don't tell them, *I* will."

Parmiter followed him out to the living room. Jamis opened the door and was about to step out when his eyes fell on something outside on the small stone walk. Under the pale wash of the porch light, a *parmitera* lay on the path. It instantly rushed into the grass of the lawn.

"One of the females," said Parmiter. "I expect all twenty-eight are out there somewhere."

"You've got until tomorrow, Parmiter." Jamis walked away to his car. He stayed in the exact center of the walk, his eyes nervously fixed on the flagstones beneath.

Parmiter waited till Jamis' car had driven away. He looked up at the cool moon and smelled the night air. Then he went back to the study.

It had not worked. Jamis had been impressed, but he had opened the spectacle of Linden and King and prying questions and reaching hands and daily irritations from people. He had expected it ultimately, of course, but still he recoiled at the thought.

"Bowl," said Parmiter.

He counted them as they placidly crawled in.

Forty-five. Forty-five males accounted for. . . . Five males suddenly unaccounted for.

"Wall," said Parmiter harshly.

When they were up, he said, "Five of you are missing, correct?"

5.

"Where are they?"

GONE.

"Gone where?"

The roaches flowed silently, smoothly, across the wall like a pattern or kaleidoscope dissolving into different pictures. The word appeared almost immediately, unencumbered by any hesitant emotions. KILL.

Parmiter slumped clumsily down in his chair; the room seemed to screech and spin around the bugs. "Bowl!" he said.

The brown, whiskered bodies climbed into the bowl and waited for his next move.

Parmiter feverishly wired the bowl shut. They had overheard Jamis. Survival, survival! Jamis was a threat.

Then Parmiter sat down and frantically dialed the number of Jamis' house.

While driving through the sleeping town, Jamis thought hard about the Hephaestus Plague and James Parmiter. He wanted to blow the lid on him, even have him committed if possible. The trouble was Parmiter could only be accounted mad if he *imagined* he had spoken with insects. The fact that he had, made him the opposite of mad. It made him sane in a superior way to everybody.

The image of the roaches on the wall faded and reappeared on his retina like the latent ghosts on a cooling television tube. Each time Jamis blinked they came in stronger.

When he turned off onto Summit Avenue, Jamis had grimly decided to go ahead and publicize Parmiter's work with or without his permission. Force the issue, as it were.

The fact that the plague had abated across the country was most unreassuring. Too much damage and horror had been done already. Parmiter could not be left alone to continue his work without close official supervision. If the insects got loose again, particularly stabilized ones that bred normally, and ate normally, the . . .

Jamis pumped his brake. The car rolled past the red light and halted in the intersection. A police car pulled up beside him. "Trouble?"

"Hope not!" Jamis replied. The brake was very weak. Jamis touched the accelerator to get clear of the intersection and discovered that his power steering had died also. His car lumbered to the curb and bumped helplessly up on it.

Then Jamis sniffed. Burned rubber. Burned insulation. Burned plastic. A slight curl of smoke from under the hood. The power windows lowered silently of their own accord, the hydraulic fluid leaking into a trickle onto the gutter.

Jamis cut off the engine. He and the police heard the chirps underneath the hood.

The cop yelled, "Mister, scram out of that car, *fast!* It's full of roaches! Git!"

The cop was already wresting a hand speaker from the dash and plugging it into the output. Jamis stumbled from the car. His foot splashed in something on the asphalt. Gasoline.

The cop put on the ultrasonics. "Come on, *git!*" He swept the speaker beam from hood to tail of Jamis' car as the director slammed the door.

The ultrasonics awakened a dog in the dark house across the sidewalk. The beast set up a frantic howl and scratched at the front door. The sweep of the beam caught Jamis full on the body for just an instant. He felt a pile driver slam through his ears and explode glittering multisaws into metal fragments in his brain. His face felt a sheet of flame touch it as his skin temperature leaped. His eyes lost focus and his balance tilted him backwards against the car.

The cop cursed, realizing what he had done. He cut off the silent weapon and opened his door to jump out and assist Jamis. There was a loud *whoomph* like an invisible breath being loudly exhaled.

The fumes surrounding the car ignited, transmuting the air into a bubble of fire that froze Jamis' dazed expression into one staring rather surprised at eternity.

When the gas tank exploded, the car was kicked forward, a blossom of snapping, gnashing flames swallowing it in great, leaping gulps. The policeman made a move forward toward the dim figure deep within the flames, then wisely decided it was too late.

Parmiter waited in the church until the priest and guests had all moved out to the lawn. Then he reluctantly went out to shake Katrina Jamis' hand and give her Jamis' briefcase. "I'm sorry," he said to her.

She nodded.

"He left this. I guess he brought it over by instinct." Parmiter offered it to her.

"He carried it everywhere." She looked from it to his face. There was doubt there of a gentle sort but nevertheless searing enough to make Parmiter duck his head, mumble a good-bye, and walk stiffly away through the small groupings of professors who either nodded curtly at him or ignored him altogether.

Once he was on Forest Avenue, Parmiter loosened his tie and walked rapidly.

"James! James. Just a minute." Hallowell's long scurrying figure puffed up to him. "I'd like to walk with you, if you don't mind."

Saying that he did mind would only make more problems for Parmiter, so he merely nodded and let Hallowell walk him down the street.

"Pity," said Hallowell.

"Yes."

"Damned strange bugs. I guess things like this will be happening for some time yet. Till they're all killed off I mean."

"Freakish accident. It pays to be safe."

"Um. How come he was at your place at three in the morning?"

"My fault."

"Oh?"

"I called him over. I'd been trying to get him all day. He wanted me to do some paper for him at the Alumni Meeting, and I didn't finish it till late. He was leaving next morning."

"Ah."

"Why?"

"Was there anything in that paper that might be of interest in general, James?"

Parmiter stopped, frowning. This was too much. "David, I do wish you'd get to the point! Just ask me what you want to ask me?"

"You know they turn the speakers off at night around here, except for police cars. No one has spotted the roaches in a month or so and then suddenly boom! Ernest is dead."

"So?"

"I suppose, James, if there was any possibility they could have bred, survived the winter—in fact, God help us, formed a second generation—you'd know, wouldn't you?"

"Not necessarily. Not immediately anyhow."

Hallowell's long face became longer. "The police didn't find any carcasses of the insects in the car. They checked the exhaust, everywhere, and nothing. There's no way they could have avoided the policeman's speaker and they don't burn up. We're all taking it for granted they cannot breed, but I wonder if that's not a mistake."

Parmiter felt relieved. "It's unlikely."

"After all, a lot of people were wrong about whether they could travel in the first place, James."

"That was different."

"Not really, if you think about it."

Parmiter stopped at the corner of Forest Avenue. "I'm going this way. I guess I'll see you tomorrow."

"Yes." Hallowell still seemed bothered. "Why don't you get in touch with that Raleigh fellow. See if he's doing anything."

"Good-bye, David." Parmiter turned and walked off down the street.

The five soldiers had concealed themselves in Jamis' car, probably guided by the females in the lawn who had seen him come out of it, and commenced tearing at anything that would catch fire—brake linings, wires, and finally the gas tank, probably by way of the fuel pump.

The soldiers were back in the bowl now. Parmiter had noticed them the next day. He did not know how they had got into his house. They had come halfway across town, probably guided by chirps from those same females.

To the roaches on the wall he asked the question he had asked dozens of times before and to which he had received the same enigmatic answer.

"Why did you kill him?" he whispered.

DIE.

"Not you. I'm taking care of you."

NO.

"I am. Jamis would not have hurt you."

DIE.

"You cannot kill people! You cannot!" And Parmiter hit his fist on the table. The roaches gave no answer. They were doubtlessly confused. Death was nothing to them, merely a bumpy part of life. Even pain did not matter.

"Bowl," said Parmiter.

He fell asleep on the living room sofa. And dreamed.

Exhaustion. Strange surfaces with crazed and jumbled horizons. He felt the awful impetus of unformed, gabbling life awaiting full maturation, and the feeling pushed so deeply into him that resistance was ludicrous. Parmiter tossed in his sleep under the great, tired journey and suddenly awoke.

The singing died away, the last thrashing of the shrieks still squirmed in the corners of the vibrating house. A sharp smell of fused tin crusted with dust hung in the air from the screen over the bowl. In the center was a hole ringed with melted curlings, where the roaches had melted their way out. All were gone.

Parmiter looked hopelessly out the kitchen window at the backyard. Confidence returned to him. He was a part of their existence. They would be back. After nine days—the time it took for the eggs to hatch.

Part 3

LATE WINTER

March 2

IN the morning Parmiter called the school and told them he had the flu and would be out for a while, then he went to the supermarket and stocked up for five days. He decided the house needed cleaning, although he had been the only one in it for some time. He changed the bedsheets, swept up the broken bottles, food containers, paper wrappings, and milk cartons into the trash can. He unplugged the hot plate and cleaned it in the sink. By the time he had finished it was eleven o'clock and he was dog-tired.

March 3

PARMITER formally made out a schedule for himself. In the mornings he decided to go into the front yard and sprinkle ash around. He was so thorough about it that it exhausted him. He peered into the grass for burn spots and found nothing but stains on his clothes from the ash and grass when he stood up. In the afternoon he did the same for the backyard. No *parmiteras*.

He went into the basement and brought Clarence up and released him into the grass. The roach had served his purpose and was nearly dead. He lumbered helplessly in the fresh air and sunlight and finally disappeared into the lawn.

March 4

AT eight in the morning the phone woke him. Parmiter cursed and reminded himself to unplug it again. It was Professor Hallowell, who was sitting in for Jamis until a replacement could be found. "I'm glad I got you, Doctor Parmiter. How are you feeling today?"

"Terrible."

"Are you taking anything?"

"Pills and slop. I think it's making me sicker."

"Will you be in for class today?"

"No, I'm not well, Hallowell."

"Very well. Call me once a day, would you, Parmiter, and let us know how you're doing." Hallowell hung up without saying good-bye.

Parmiter checked the ground again that afternoon. He looked up from the grass to see that his next door neighbor, a man with a bald bullet head named Emmet Larch, was standing on his back porch watching Parmiter poke through the grass.

"Lose something?" asked Emmet Larch.

"Yes," answered Parmiter, "a rare coin."

"Need any help?"

"No, I don't."

When evening fell, Parmiter went into the house, fixed a TV dinner and a bowl of soup, then settled down to watch television. Tomorrow he would start on a monograph describing the roaches.

March 5

EMMET LARCH said, "I really feel like an idiot, you know. I didn't want to bother you, but the missus remembered you worked at the school and knew all about bugs, and they named the fire beetles after you, so here I am."

Stifling a yawn, Parmiter stepped aside to let Larch inside. In Larch's hand was a tin coffee can which he set uneasily on the coffee table when he sat down. "Ethel said you was probably busy working for the government and writing books and stuff and flying off to see the President. She wanted me to come over here and feed you or some damn thing. Ethel, I told her, leave the man alone, I said. Right?"

"Exactly," said Parmiter, pouring out coffee for him.

"Anyhow she did some readin' and she says, 'Emmet, dog if that man didn't kill them bugs off and save this country.' That true?"

"No." Parmiter laughed.

"Can I shake your hand anyhow?"

Parmiter wiped his hand and nervously extended it to Larch, who shook it powerfully.

"There! I done it." Larch beamed in admiration at Parmiter, who felt strangely pleased and even more strangely tearful, not out of shyness but from a deeper feeling that could only be reached by somebody innocent. He felt at these times that there was so much he wanted to warn people about, so much he could tell.

"Don't flatter me, Mr. Larch."

"Naw . . . come on, please. Emmet!"

"All right, Emmet. What's on your mind?"

"Yeah, well, I thought you might be interested in this bug. It's really something. Ethel found it in the basement and hollered like a beagle. We figured it was one of them fire things 'cause it was hard as iron. Here now." Larch flipped off the coffee can cover.

Parmiter looked at the insect. It was a dead *parmitera*. A small one. A worker. "It's a cockroach, Mr. Larch."

"Uh huh."

"Just powder the basement. Or spray it. That'll get rid of them."

"They gonna be all over the place?"

"Hope not."

Larch stood and held out his hand again. "Say, uh, Jim. Don't suppose you play poker?"

"No, I don't."

"Oh, well, I guess we haven't said more than five words to each other long as you been here. You come see us, y'hear?"

Parmiter checked his own basement. Nothing. They were in the neighborhood all right. The trick was to check around without being seen by Emmet Larch.

When night pressed in on him, Parmiter watched television again. He caught a late horror movie titled *X, the Unknown*. It was about a huge gob of slithering mud that ate radiation and melted people in England. It melted two children, one country church, two National Servicemen, and one horny intern. A brilliant scientist turned it into detergent with radar screens. It was great. Parmiter loved it.

March 6

HE called Hallowell again.

"Still sick?" the professor asked incredulously. "I hope you're not dying."

"I feel like it."

"Will you be in Monday?"

"Probably not."

"Very well." Hallowell did not believe him, but there was nothing he could do.

On the front lawn Parmiter found one small burned spot of grass.

In the afternoon Parmiter began his monograph. He gathered together tapes, test results, Metbaum's papers, and Miss Denton's locustine thesis (both of them with the names of the authors prominent), and the carbon copies of the tests the Raleigh pathology lab and King's lab had sent to him. After an hour of writing laboriously in longhand, Parmiter found the going rough.

Saturday, March 7

ON the lawns he found more burned patches but no insects. He wrote all day long while buried safely in his study with the curtains drawn.

March 8

EMMET LARCH appeared in the doorway, holding a jar of marmalade his wife had made up especially for Parmiter. "Ethel just wanted to send this over as thanks for getting those bugs out of the house."

"I didn't get any bugs out of your house, Larch. Leave me alone and take that . . . stuff with you!" Parmiter slammed the door in Emmet Larch's face.

He was in a foul mood, but not out of frustration so much as fear.

The insects should be numerous now, at least around the house, and yet it was flawlessly clean, upstairs and down.

The mail had brought requests from two magazines for Parmiter to write about the roaches and a request from a writer for an interview on his retrospective thoughts about the plague last fall. He sent back three one-word notes: No.

The constant tension had made him tired, so he took a nap on the living room sofa and dreamed about Rome and Sparta again. Whatever it was he was after, the dream almost gave it to him. Parmiter dreamed of tiny skeletons on bleak hillsides, piles of them, surrounded by empty wastes, with cities rotting into ruin.

Parmiter slept six straight hours and awoke at seven fifteen. Out of the previous twenty-four hours he had slept eighteen. He only overslept when he was frightened. The dream was enough to frighten a raging leopard. Yet its harsh images almost closed the facts about the *parmiteras* in his head. It was on the tip of his mind.

Parmiter walked around the town that night, trying to figure out his dream, but it was hopeless. It would come when it was good and ready. The moon was high and heavy, and the air was filled with crickets and night birds. He had forgotten how good it was to get out of the house.

At ten that night there was a knock on his door. It was a student whom he had never seen before. "Hallowell sent me over with this, Doctor. He wondered if you could identify it."

The boy opened a glass jar. Inside was a *parmitera*.

"Where did he find it?"

"His basement, sir. He said he saw several."

Parmiter felt his stomach sink. Hallowell lived several blocks away on Summit Avenue. The bugs' sense of environment, which included him as its most secure point, was breaking up. "It's a cockroach. It's harmless, but tell Hallowell to spray it. Why did he send you?"

"Oh, I live around here, Doc."

After the boy left, Parmiter tried to write some more but could not.

They had spread all over town. He had not anticipated that. His fear deepened.

PARMITER'S yards were covered with burned spots but no *parmiteras.* He looked over and saw some in Emmet Larch's yard also.

Parmiter stayed outside all day. He walked around the block and for the first time in his life noticed the houses of his neighbors. Across from him was a huge tree-shrouded house with flower-filled stone vases in the front yard. A wealthy man named Fincher owned it, and every spring he invited dozens of people over for barbecues and a stroll about the yard under the cool evenings.

Afternoon found Parmiter still agitatedly walking around outdoors. Tomorrow. What the hell were they doing in Larch's yard? Why weren't they in *his* yard?

Evening. Someone was burning leaves down the block, and the smoke mixed with the damp smell of the grass. A good neighborhood. Civilized. Clean. The spark of a pipe materialized beside him. It was Larch.

Parmiter hastily said, "Mr. Larch, you must forgive my temper the other morning. I *am* sorry."

Larch shrugged, but Parmiter could not tell if his feelings had been assuaged. "Feels good out here long about eight," he said.

"Yes, it certainly does, Mr. Larch, it does."

"Emmet."

"Yes. Emmet."

"Come on over and sit in the yard. I'll get us a beer."

"I was on my way inside, Emmet. But thanks."

Larch played with his pipe. "Remember that bug I showed you? Basement's crawling with them; they're stacked three deep. Ethel liked to went crazy." He motioned with his pipe, taking in the entire street. "Yeah, we all got a bug problem. Fred Hepman killed a bunch the other day. And Fincher over there across the street. Block is full of them. Damn glad it isn't any of your fire bastards . . . You feeling okay, Jim?"

Parmiter had swayed slightly and grabbed Larch for support. The insects could not have bred that fast unless . . . Madilene's egg case had hatched some that had not come into the basement in the first place. Suppose there had always been more than eighty-two waiting out here, perhaps under the winter snow?

"Emmet, these bugs. Are they doing anything . . . odd?"

Larch thought a moment, then replied, "Yeah, actually. There's always one in the bedroom in the morning. Gives Ethel the creeps. He sits there watchin' us, then takes off soon as I get the spray. . . ."

Dear God, what was going on?

March 10

HE had not slept in twenty-four hours. He needed a shave. He sat at his desk feverishly writing from the notes he had made on the *parmiteras,* the experiments, behavior and characteristics. He did not know what else to do. He had checked the house from top to bottom and found nothing. Burned spots were all over the grass in front, and that morning he had seen Fincher across the street curiously examining his lawn.

Just before going into his house the previous night, just after Larch had left, Parmiter heard a low buzz under the cries of the crickets threading through the night. An answering chorus of buzzes had sounded from several points all along the street. The houses slept in the night.

Parmiter had run inside and locked the door. Larch had shaken his head sadly, thinking Parmiter had to throw up. Parmiter had gathered all his haphazard notes together. He had to put it in writing. And then he had collided with Rome and Sparta again. The idea would still not show itself. Today was the ninth day.

Now it was night again, a final night, and only he knew it.

Parmiter methodically wrote the sheets of yellow paper because he did not know what else he could do. There was nobody he could call, nobody he could share this impending moment with, whatever it would be.

A kind of loneliness had impelled him to plug his phone in again and see what would happen. He got a blizzard of phone calls from neighbors whom he had met years before, from Hepman, Fincher, and, of course, Larch, complaining about bugs in their houses.

It was not fair, Parmiter thought. He had helped their birth; they had depended on him. Now they were betraying him. It was immoral. And suddenly Parmiter understood Rome and Sparta and what it meant to him. He was writing it down before he realized it. It was, he believed, a discovery to rank with any theoretical proposition in the century.

I wish, at the conclusion of this work, to put forward a hypothesis concerning survival, which I believe to be the only law of nature directly connected to a human ethic.

The survival of any species is solely dependent on how it cares for its offspring.

The salmon lays eggs by the thousands and so cares for his breed, insuring their numbers. This is no less solicitous than the kangaroo that cares for one or two infants at a time in her pouch. The fly that leaves maggots cares for its offspring simply by assuring there are so many of them.

This is a thesis that may seem self-evident until one looks closely at its implications. I believe this drive to be superior to the sex and hunger drive in all species including man. I believe it accounts for the instinctive tenderness man feels for younger creatures—kittens, puppies, even eggs—and which disappears once the infant has reached adulthood.

This response to the young is found in all living creatures and is directly comparable to the human response of sacrifice and its corollaries which are considered the most civilized of capabilities. Sacrifice is impossible in a creature that does not possess the sense of compassion or the ideals of generosity and the concurrent ability to sublimate its own immediate wellbeing for the sake of another. In humans this ability is extended not just to the young but to others of its kind.

I believe it to be an instinct rather than an ideal, a drive rather than a conscious act. . . .

Parmiter found that his writing was imprecise and meandering. He put down his pen and stretched. He was almost there. He looked at his watch. It was seven fifteen.

They came into the house silently in complete possession of it. They came through the joints in the walls, sifting in from the grass, through innumerable cracks in plumbing, plaster, and wood—all the myriad faults that no human eye would bother to detect.

Parmiter looked up from the monograph to the bookcase. Perched there was a soldier roach surveying him. From the hall came a scratching—pervasive, irresistible—of thousands of feet. Parmiter looked in dread. The column was three feet wide. They were on the walls and ceiling, all marching silently toward the cellar door.

"Stop!" he cried, getting to his feet.

Two chirps.

"Yes!"

Two chirps.

Parmiter had just finished writing about locustine. Perhaps that was part of the explanation. An accelerated birth rate. Put them all together, crowd them, and watch them explode in numbers.

He ran into the kitchen for the spray can. The column halted, then whipped, roiling around like a snake reversing itself. The chirping rose like a wave as the insects formed a circle around his legs.

"Wall," commanded Parmiter.

A hundred of them ran up the wall.

"How many are you?"

MANY.

He set the spray can down. He put out the lights. The ticking of the bugs whispered through the house. The circle surrounding him broke up and continued into the hall. They merged beneath the basement door, continuing down.

Parmiter put out all the houselights. He looked out the living room window at the night. He saw soft streetlamps in the evening before sleepy yellow-windowed houses. He sniffed the air. Then he drew the shade and followed them down into the basement.

Normally the basement had beige walls and a gray stone floor.

Tonight the walls and floor were black and undulated like a carpet beneath the swarming bodies of the bugs. They roiled off the surfaces and coated the ceiling. They turned hard-edged objects, desk corners, steps, pipe joints, moldings into rounded scaly lumps with their gigantic presence.

They parted for his feet as Parmiter made his way down the steps and closed over his path as he passed by. He tried to examine them as he walked. Same long antennae, same hard shells. The species seemed fixed. They cleared a spot from the wall then several rushed in to spell out words.

JAMES PARMITER.

"Where is Clarence?" he cried.

DEAD.

"How?"

EAT.

"Oh, God." He nearly fainted. Be calm, be calm . . . "Are you all in this house tonight? Spell it out."

NO.

"Where are the rest?"

NEAR.

"Other houses? Homes?"

YES.

Parmiter's voice became husky with combined fear and resentment. He looked at the black legions swirling around him. No human in history had ever beheld such a moment, *never!* And yet his only feeling was resentment that he had miscalculated their behavior. Why did they not come back sooner? On such pettiness, the gods laughed. He was experiencing true existentialist absurdity. No Gabriel's trumpet, no new era for mankind. Just a dried-out thirty-five-year-old snotty academic in a basement in a hack Southern college.

"What are you going to do?"

HOME.

"I don't understand. You're not behaving as you should! You should depend on me! You belong to me! I am your origin and you try to dominate me! You are not an accident, you are a calculated creation of mine . . . and you are making me *mad!* Mad, I tell you!"

HOME.

"You *are* home!" he fairly yelled. "You're in this house and it is your home."

DARK.

There was a pervasive, uncertain rustle among them. The word was not right, and many more roaches swarmed onto the wall. Parmiter saw occasional letters flit like thoughts across its surface. Then the word came back, stronger than ever.

DARK.

He said slowly, "This place is dark. Many insects are nocturnal. The dark never bothered you all before. *Where* is home?"

BELOW.

He had it then! It needed no elaboration. Parmiter was flabbergasted. "For God's sake, you don't mean underground! You mean back into the chasm."

YES.

The bacteria. That was who he was talking to. It was the microbes that wanted to return underground. The perfect host-parasite relationship. The microbes have the memory; the insects have the bodies. The microbes.

A word appeared: HELP.

"That chasm is a hundred miles south of here, down in Candor. Go on! Go back home!"

NEED HELP.

"All right, all right." There were so many things he wished to know. He should be prostrate with terror, but he had to ask, to learn! "Listen to me, listen now! Have you ever communicated with other humans before me? Ever?"

YES.

Outrageous! So much work! He thought he had their sole allegiance. "When?"

A number formed, the last three digits of which wavered, dissolved, and refocused. They knew written numbers only from his doodles and mutterings. Accuracy was impossible.

100000000.

"Years, you mean?"

YES.

"Did they speak to you like me?"

YES.

"Neanderthals maybe. Cro-Magnon. Pre-Homo sapiens. Yes. You undoubtedly lived in the Ice Age. Let me think! Yes. You probably did not talk in language, but you got along well through something else. Grunts, perhaps. What a silly thing to say! Sorry. Was it speech? Answer me, did they speak language to you! Answer me!"

YES.

"Ah! Good. You were acquainted with language before me. You were a constant companion of early man and your genes remember this. What about writing? Did you know writing? Writing would bring you up to civilized times. . . ."

HOME.

"Writing! Answer me! Did you know writing?"

NO.

Upstairs the door chimes rang, vibrating through the house. "Mr. Parmiter? Mr. Parmiter! I brought you some hot chili. Do you hear me?"

NO NO NO.

It was Mrs. Larch with some food.

"Go away!" Parmiter shouted. "Go away!"

The chimes rang again.

HOME.

Parmiter directed his command to the hundreds of roaches on the floor blocking his way to the door. "Wall," he cried. They did not move.

HOME.

"Mr. Parmiter, I hear you. Are you all right?"

Parmiter tried to balance his tensions. A cool rage might make them know who he was, but his voice was not cool—it was cold. Cold, harsh, cutting, and final. "I cannot take you home! I am not a god; life does not have a home! Wherever it lives is home. I can do nothing more for you ever again!"

A quiet, charged moment of impending great events. . . .

The shattering, thunderous chirping erupted like a concussion bomb that shattered the house to its granite foundations.

The roaches had infested the rest of the house as well as the basement. The entire place was an oven before Parmiter made it up the stairs. Filthy gray smoke ballooned through the stone basement, partially obscuring the dirty flames that outlined every flammable object—boxes, tables, chairs, plywood walls, and the wooden stairs up which he frantically clawed, and finally the wall of fire which was the door itself.

Parmiter felt his clothes incinerate and his flesh blister. Each step up the stairs tilted his balance and plunged his sense deeper into the roaring din. He thought he heard a woman scream. Then shouts. The fire ate deeper into his body, squeezing the sanity out and letting the floods of agony in.

His agony saved him in the end, as he screamed, thrashed, and bludgeoned his way through melting wood, thinking all the while that this was not James Parmiter making a fool of himself, not this sad little man living his life backwards and dying in his own basement. James Parmiter could not conceivably be *that* stupid.

Emmet Larch pulled Parmiter's steaming body from the house to the sidewalk. It was but one of the heroic acts that were lost in the inferno that engulfed Bainboro and the county that night. Dumb, sincere, shy Emmet Larch left Parmiter's blackened body on the sidewalk and plunged into the burning timbers of Parmiter's house just on the off-chance that his wife was still alive.

March 23

THE sea. It undulated and swelled gracefully into silver walls that subsided into blackness. Sometimes the silver rose out of control in a dazzling wall of white that threatened to swallow him. They told Parmiter his heart was failing at those times.

A last wave massed and piled itself up, lifting him higher and higher until Parmiter found himself whimpering in terror at a white ceiling with an inset, fluorescent light. Then the wave loosened beneath him and he was awake at last. He was wrapped and safety-pinned in a gleaming white bed under brilliant white sheets.

The suspended ball of haze over him finally, after two days of wavering, focused into a face. Metbaum. Parmiter tried to speak and Metbaum bent down to listen, but the only sounds were groans.

Metbaum said to the doctor, "How come he doesn't talk? I know he recognizes me."

"Traumatic shock," answered the doctor. "We're moving him out of that room. We had to go on emergency power last night you know. Some wiring was burned by the roaches."

For two weeks Parmiter had been in a room where flowers were changed daily. He had been awake but traumatized. The nurses passing in and out bothered him, interrupted his concentration. People whom he had not wanted to see kept coming in and speaking to him. Wiley King. Max Linden. A man named Reynolds.

Sometimes Parmiter heard sirens, and he would look out the window, but he could see only a smudge of smoke in the distance, beyond the tree line.

Parmiter had not spoken a single word for two weeks, even though he was conscious. He did not answer nurses who asked him how he felt, and he had not answered Metbaum who talked incessantly about nothing. But he did notice how Metbaum clammed up whenever Linden entered with flowers.

March 24

PARMITER said clearly, "Metbaum?"

Metbaum's eyes narrowed. He got up and silently closed the door. "Okay, Doc. I hear you."

"What's been happening to me?"

"Don't you know?"

"I wouldn't ask if I did, damn it all."

"Doc. Relax. I'm getting a doctor." Metbaum left and returned with an intern who listened to Parmiter's heart, checked his blood pressure, and took his temperature. "You have ten minutes to talk. After that, he sleeps."

Metbaum watched the doctor go out. "You don't remember the roaches? The *parmiteras?*" he asked as soon as the door closed.

Fire. Horror. Screams. Legions of insects and words on the wall. Parmiter began trembling. "The roaches . . . the roaches. . . ."

"Easy, Doc . . ." Metbaum's eyes became alarmed. "Come on. . . ."

"Metbaum, destroy that tank. . . ."

Metbaum's eyes ignited with fear. He whispered loudly, "Stop it! Don't mention that . . ."

Metbaum pushed the emergency bell and some nurses came in to give Parmiter an injection.

Lounging outside in the hall was Wiley King.

Parmiter's voice rose. "Kill them! They're loose! Metbaum, they're coming out of the tank. . . ."

One of the nurses firmly pushed Metbaum out of the door next to Wiley King. She slammed the door behind her. King looked inquiringly at the student. "I thought you said he was better."

"Physically he is; mentally he's in some kind of trauma. What do I know? His consciousness is holding something back that doesn't want to stay back."

They talked while walking down the hall and found Linden sitting in the reception area. Linden had a bunch of flowers in his hand. He glanced self-consciously down at them. "I thought you said he was better, Metbaum." Metbaum explained it all over again.

King asked, "Mr. Metbaum, he said something about them coming out of a tank. There may be something there."

Metbaum said, "No. There's nothing to that."

"He was very positive. . . ."

"No, no, he meant the oil burner in his basement or something."

King asked, "You didn't use any sterile tanks or anything when you were working with them, did you? Think now."

Metbaum thought hard for a few minutes. "No. He must have meant the oil burner or something. We never used any kind of tank or anything like that." Metbaum loudly blew his nose. "Christ, now I'm getting a cold."

They walked out to King's car. Metbaum said, "I think I'll hang around for a while."

King started the car and slowly pulled out of the graveled drive toward the Bainboro campus, which by now should have been showing leaves but was, like the town, a burned, smoking wreck.

Metbaum walked back into the hospital and sat down in his seat. A nurse passed him and said, "Want something to eat?"

"No."

"You can go on home, you know. We'll call you when he gets better."

"No," said Metbaum. "I want to be the first to see him. I want him to know I'm here."

March 25

WHEN Parmiter's eyes opened, they were bright, clear, and alert. They took in the room, his own injuries, and the figure seated at the door. "Metbaum. You still here?"

"Yes."

"What's been happening?"

"They came back in the spring. To put it mildly. It's a subspecies of some kind, restricted to this state. There are fires all over the place. It's a second generation of some kind and they're raising hell. They must have been hibernating or something. The Air Force is using combat copters to spray the towns and woods. Every night some place burns up in Bainboro. That's what's happening."

Parmiter said, "How?"

"It started here. We think it could have been some of our lab samples, but what the hell. . . ." Metbaum droned on, recounting catastrophes. "They were putting up tent cities in the countryside and planning emergency food drops."

A peculiar feeling came over Parmiter. He felt that he was going to die any minute now. Truth had been compressed in him for so long that, like a spring on which the latches were giving way, it would explode in a cataclysmic eruption. "Metbaum! Metbaum! I did it! I killed those people! God help me, God help me! I killed them all . . . I did it. . . ."

The dials monitoring his vital functions leaped.

Metbaum said, "Shut up. Somebody's coming."

Parmiter felt a wave build beneath him, the swell of the sea.

The doctor came in and gave Parmiter a shot. He looked down at the weeping entomologist as the drug slowly took hold. Finally he was asleep. The doctor asked, "What happened?"

Metbaum snapped, "He remembered the fire. He'll be okay." He turned and walked out of the room, slamming the door. The doctor watched Metbaum go. The boy was tired. He had never spoken to him like that before.

The sirens woke Parmiter again. He pressed his bell and a nurse came in. He whispered loudly, "Is Metbaum still here?"

She nodded.

"Get him. I have to talk to him."

Metbaum pulled his chair up close to the bed and listened to the dry, pain-wracked voice in silence. When Parmiter finished, Metbaum's face was white. "It's not possible."

"It happened, Metbaum, it happened! Jamis saw them!" Parmiter held tightly to his assistant's sleeve. "Listen, Metbaum! There's a monograph on my table in the den. It's all there, all my notes, everything. I had a theory, Metbaum, a big one about . . . I can't remember. You must get my notes."

"They burned up along with the house, Doc," said Metbaum coldly.

"Burned . . . *up!*"

"Everything. Along with the block. It's not possible. . . ."

"I told you, Metbaum, I told you they had potentials . . . Burned up. . . ." Parmiter lay back against the pillow and fell asleep again. Then, just as suddenly, he awoke once more. "You say the insects are moving south?"

"Yes."

"I know where they're going. The sand hills. The chasm. You must help me get out of here. Will you help me?"

Metbaum answered bitterly, "I'm in it up to my neck," but Parmiter had dropped off again.

March 26

LINDEN and King came to the hospital to take Parmiter out for the day. The doctor strapped him into a wheelchair. Metbaum followed but said nothing during the whole tour.

They wheeled Parmiter across campus to what had been Carson Hall. Parmiter shivered at the landscape, which resembled a Bosch painting. The grass was a layer of charcoal, the town buildings were black-streaked shells, and the trees were all scorched and gnarled like black birds fallen to earth. Trucks with protruding insecticide nozzles patrolled the streets. The smell made Parmiter gag.

The Institute for Short-Lived Phenomena had helped set up a lab in Carson Hall, the brick wing that had not burned to the ground. It was on the first floor. The officials from Raleigh and Washington talked in urgent, low tones about parathion and other poisons.

Linden wheeled Parmiter into a room stacked with debris from his own house. There lay his old yearbook, a camera, some soaked magazines, and his hot plate. On the table also was the diving helmet. It was bent out of shape and cracked from the fire.

Linden said, "The police checked through your house for valuables, James, as a favor to me. They knew about your work with the sound waves. I'm terribly sorry, but we didn't find much."

"Thank you anyway."

"We found this helmet next to a compressor."

Parmiter shook his head impatiently. "Picked them up years ago. Toys. Throw them out."

Linden, still smiling, looked at Metbaum with what Metbaum thought was sharpness, then back at Parmiter. "James, we couldn't save much. We were looking to see if you had any files on *Hephaestus parmitera* we hadn't seen before. They're behaving very oddly. You see, the plague originated in this town and has been spreading in one general direction. None of them have moved north or even tried to leave the state. They apparently mated with one of our earthbound species. The bacteria in them has moved into the brain. King has isolated a nucleoside from the bacteria with an electron microscope. We've been checking the stuff with Metbaum's blood too." He smiled at Metbaum who did not react.

"James, do you know anything about these creatures? Where the hell did they come from?"

"Lab samples that escaped back in the fall," said Parmiter.

"How did they breed though?"

"God knows."

Linden bit his lip and thought a moment. "They seem to be migrating. I don't know who's winning, them or us. We're killing them by the thousands with spray, but they just keep coming."

When they took Parmiter back to the hospital, Metbaum lingered behind as Linden, King, and the doctor left.

After the door closed, Parmiter delicately swung his legs onto the floor and, to Metbaum's shock, stood up on his feet. "Not bad eh?" he said. "Chalk it up to desperation."

He sat back down on the bed, sweat beading his forehead as the pain subsided to a dull ache. "Tonight, Metbaum. Bring your car around and help me get out. We're going south."

"South to where?"

"Candor. They haven't gotten down there yet but it's just a matter of two or three days. Besides they found the pressure tank. We'll both be in for it if we don't move tonight."

Parmiter lay down on the bed and Metbaum returned to the waiting room to continue his vigil.

Parmiter tried to sleep for the next two hours but kept dreaming of the great silver wave again. He forced himself awake before it could cover him and heard a siren echoing across the night.

He listened to his room. He heard the nurse's footsteps answering a patient's bell down the hall. He breathed deeply and felt the wave still inside him even while awake.

The wave was always there, growing in him. A psychiatrist could probably explain it, but Parmiter realized he did not want to know what it meant. He got out of bed and walked quietly around the room. It made him feel better even though his burns were still sore. Moving around made the wave subside within him.

He sat on the bed feeling the conflicts of exhaustion and the wave. He twisted a corner of the bedsheet around in his hand. Then he got up and very slowly began to pull his pants on over his bandages. It made him feel much better. Action. Control. Grasp your destiny! That was what he believed in. He could not let Metbaum blow up the chasm; he would never be rid of the wave for the rest of his life.

Parmiter glanced in the mirror and was shocked to see tears on his cheeks.

He was losing control. He must not do that.

March 27

AT two in the morning Metbaum's car was backed up against the laundry entrance. He had remained in the waiting room as the nurse read a paperback. The light on her board blinked and she said, "I'll be in Five F in case of any trouble."

When she left, the hall was empty. Metbaum entered Parmiter's room and saw the entomologist tightening a belt over his pants. Then he painfully tucked the shirt in over the bandages.

He half carried, half walked Parmiter down the stairwell, out to the car. Parmiter sank down in the front seat with a sigh of relief.

They cruised slowly through Bainboro. Rows of empty burned houses watched them silently, and the car bumped over chunks of black wood from the trees. Most of the rubbish had been swept into small piles that lined the streets.

In the countryside, moonlight glinted through the blackened, blasted trees. Every now and then in the distance they could make out glowing after-fires and the figures of men beating at them with blankets. Along the paved roads the sight was even more incredible. Trailers and tents were pitched in fields of ash surrounded by the remnants of forests. They could hear thin music coming from radios inside the tents.

After ten miles they passed a truck full of soldiers going toward Bainboro. Spray gun nozzles were stacked between them.

The silent black Chevrolet, the same car Metbaum and Parmiter had driven down to the sandhills long ago to find the first roaches, cruised on under the cold moon shining down on the wasted land, a huge metal bug itself.

"Turn on the news, Metbaum."

The radio said the bugs had hit Goldsboro earlier that evening. The county was burning. Then came the real horror. The roaches were attacking people when nothing else flammable was available.

"Christ," muttered Metbaum.

"It's the insecticide. It's working too well. The roaches now consider man a natural enemy."

"What next, Doc?"

"Next? They'll probably get cunning. They'll burn down houses to drive the people out and. . . ."

"Christ," Metbaum said again.

"We do the same thing to animals. They've just turned it around against us. They're as intelligent as we are."

Metbaum turned the dial again and found the piercing voice of the Reverend Kern Speece of Beulah Hill Baptist Church delivering a twenty-minute job.

"Brothers," Speece shouted enthusiastically," God is gettin' madder by the minute."

Montgomery and Star counties were wide awake waiting for the roaches. Insecticides were stocked in spray guns in every farm. Fire departments were on alert and firebreaks had been plowed in the fields.

At Parmiter's insistence Metbaum drove up to Henry Tacker's place and roused him out of bed. The lights in the house were on and Tacker, wearing his overalls, stepped out of the house as they stopped.

"I ain't seen any of 'em yet, but, hell, I ain't no expert. I'm ready. We're waitin' for the house to burn down around our heads, but I've sprayed the farm so much you can't hardly move without suffocatin'. Them things're walking this way, right?"

"Yes. They'll be here in about thirteen hours. I'd leave town for a while if I were you, Mr. Tacker."

"I ain't leavin' my house. I just ain't."

Parmiter looked out over the dark fields. "Is that chasm still filled up?"

"You damn right! And it's roped off too."

Henry Tacker directed them to Miss Parker's boardinghouse in Candor and rang her up to warn her they were coming.

The town had been hastily rebuilt after the original fires. Too many buildings looked out of place with clean cinder-block walls and fresh creamy wood.

Before they collapsed on the twin beds with the calico covers, Parmiter exercised slowly, touching his toes, stretching his arms and grimacing with pain.

"I must loosen myself up."

"You're weak."

"Not that weak. Metbaum, tomorrow you must buy some dynamite from somewhere around here. There's nothing to it. You're a bright boy—you can get it." Parmiter laid down on his bed.

Metbaum could not shake the terror that boiled within him. "What happens if it doesn't work? What if they don't go into the chasm?"

"Then we go back to the hospital, apologize for bothering everybody, and try again. But it will work. It will work."

When Metbaum drove over to a construction company in Pinehurst, he saw *parmiteras* on the road. There weren't many of them. They scooted rapidly out of the way of his wheels. Scouts, he decided. They were already plowing fields and spraying them.

A man named Sherits was busily packing files into a metal cabinet. "Them bugs burned up a couple of houses outside a town. Didn't you hear? You can see 'em on the streets. What you need dynamite for, boy?"

Sherits sat down heavily before a small, rotating fan and sweated profusely.

"Blasting firebreaks," said Metbaum.

"Blastin's gotta be done right if you in the city limits. You from around here?"

Metbaum said angrily, "Forget it, I'll find some somewhere else," and started for the door.

Sherits mopped his face and said, "Now hold your horses there a minute—hold on. . . ."

Metbaum was gone for only two hours. When he returned, he saw more *parmiteras* on the road and several in Candor. The local gas stations had emptied their tanks and stowed their inflammable oil.

Miss Parker told him the Grain and Feed Store had found several in the basement. She also offered them some hush puppies, which they refused.

Metbaum set the thick wrapped paper cylinder on a table. Parmiter limped over to examine it and both suddenly froze at the sound of the fire siren, hooting away in the distance.

"Volunteer firemen. Any trouble?"

"No, it's like buying soup. How are we supposed to do this? Do we ask Tacker or what?"

"Tacker wouldn't like it, Metbaum, use your head. We park on the road and then you run out into the field, plant the dynamite, and run back again. Then we drive back to Bainboro. If it works, we're heroes; if it doesn't, we apologize."

"Why don't you get to work on another monograph, Doc? We've got a couple of hours. Do an outline. . . ."

"There'll be time for that." Parmiter touched his toes. Metbaum sat on a bed, hands clasped between his legs, and looked around at the walls as if waiting for voices.

"Look alive there, Metbaum, it's almost all over. What's wrong with you?"

"I'm scared. Aren't you scared?"

"Nothing alive scares me, Metbaum."

"Don't those people mean anything to you?"

"What's dead is dead. Insects deal in it. It's nothing to be afraid of; in fact, it's a very merciful invention sometimes. Imagine a world without death, Metbaum. There wouldn't be any heaven, would there. Get some sleep. They won't be here for hours."

In spite of the insecticide and dampened buildings, the roaches hit Candor at seven o'clock as though nothing could stop them. They did not come in like tidal waves; they just appeared in places where they had not been moments before. Stores. Porches. Rooms. Depots. Within minutes they were gathering into columns like streams flowing into a river and marching down the streets. People stamped on them.

The fires began in trash barrels and corners. Then brush and finally walls. The insecticide made the flames spread. Then the sirens began.

Jordy Harris, Harmon Shull, and Henry Tacker were in Maxine Horner's house drinking boilermakers and playing their weekly poker match when the hoot of the siren pierced the air.

Maxine's phone rang. She listened for a moment, then said, "Jordy! Your house!"

Jordy folded up his flush. The others dusted off their drinks. "It figgers," Jordy muttered. "It figgers!"

The four blocks the men covered to their cars revealed a good half of Candor to them. The town was completely on fire, spreading a pall of black smoke and upward-cataract of sparks to the stars. As Jordy watched, the Grain and Feed Store erupted in a dozen corners then crashed apart in a shower of flames.

The thunder of shouts and car horns was loud but not disorganized. Jordy and his friends drove out of the town westward to the high school. That was designated an area for tents and homeless people which by now included his own family. As he drove through town, Jordy noticed a car heading east for the farmlands where his warehouse was. He thought he saw somebody familiar at the wheel and wondered if he should tell them they were going the wrong way. Then he remembered. It was that professor and the boy. They must know what they were doing.

The whooping siren faded behind Metbaum and Parmiter some seven miles into the country. Confronting them was a solid ocean of flame, a low rumble of fire from orchards, trees, and buildings, sending up waves of dirty brown smoke that bellied skyward, reflecting orange flames on the undersides of their billows.

Metbaum tapped the windshield. "Look there! Look at them!"

Clumps of roaches like dark rippling puddles huddled in the twin glares of the headlights and the fires.

A mile south of Henry Tacker's farm Metbaum could no longer see the road, just surging crawling bodies outlined by the burning brush of the fields and trees. They passed burning cars, tractors, and trailers stalled by the road. The chirping of the creatures cooed and bellowed over the land as if it were coming from the clouds.

Tacker's burning house illuminated the fields. They stopped the car and watched how the land seemed to writhe under the moon and firelight. They had passed no cars for the last several miles. The whole area was uninhabitable.

The instant he stopped Metbaum heard a thunderous chirping from the back seat. "Christ," he said, leaping into the back as smoke filled the closed car. Metbaum grabbed and kicked at the chirping bugs, coughing violently at the acrid smoke from the seats. Parmiter sat rigidly in the seat. Then quietly and painfully, since his burned arms had made his skin tight, he slid the dynamite out from the bag.

Metbaum looked at the swarms of roaches on the windows. "Hell," he said.

Parmiter's door flew open, letting in the oceanic roar of the roaches. Parmiter half rolled, half jumped out of the car and took off toward Tacker's burning house, carrying the dynamite with him.

Metbaum saw Parmiter plunge into the county-wide carpet of insects and run toward the north field where the chasm was. Metbaum slammed the door but the insects had gotten into the car. They swarmed over the seats, the roof, and the dash. He felt a thousand tickles as they rooted into the cuffs of his shirt and dug at his shoes.

Metbaum flattened the horn button and screamed at the windshield, but the closed car bounced his own voice back to him. He watched Parmiter's figure vanish in the field. Metbaum slammed into reverse. The gears wept, then screeched as he lunged back down the highway. Out the back window he saw the red glare of the taillights lighting up millions of marching, whiskered bodies rolling beneath his crushing wheels.

Tacker's driveway was some two hundred yards back, Metbaum recalled. But he could not find it. He ran the car back and forth over the stretch of highway but saw nothing but insects lit up by

Tacker's lone, burning house, which looked like the last stand of sanity against a madman's nightmare.

The insects dug at Metbaum's neck and hands, their billions of legs caressing him until he could stand it no longer. He opened the door. The roaches cascaded into the car like a soft, squirmy tidal wave. Metbaum waded out through them. He felt the hard asphalt under his feet that slid over their crushed bodies as he ran down the highway.

Suddenly something so strange happened that Metbaum could not be sure he imagined it. The chirping stopped. A wave of silence brushed across the roaches all the way to the horizon. The insects were still. The antennae were rigid. Something had passed through them. A message.

Metbaum knew of the tides running through the animal world. No one could explain them. Birds took off in entire flocks instantly as if a subsonic signal had touched them. The same was true of fish shoals. Metbaum ran on through thousands of quiet, alert bodies. They died without a movement of protest. Then his car blew up in a lazy geyser of gasoline and tumbling doors that ripped and burned through their ranks.

Then the night split with a flash of blue light that imprinted in his eyes details the dark had concealed. In the flashes Metbaum saw the outlines of the *parmiteras*—the rigid, strong bodies like torpedoes, the poised legs, and the jumble of mouth parts. They did not care about him; they could kill him as if he were a stone to walk upon or a piece of mud to pass over.

Thunderclaps from the ripping lightning passed over the waves of insects. Ripples swept by them. Metbaum knew the blasts were from dynamite, but he no longer cared. Parmiter knew what he was doing. He would get back.

The last and mightiest explosion knocked Metbaum on his face. Instantly the chirping of the roaches began again, and they flowed past him, around him, and away from him like a swirl of water caught in a whirlpool centered in Tacker's field.

Parmiter felt his feet slush around in the soft sand. He had forgotten how hard it was to run in sand, how it forced him to use all the muscles in his ankles to stay balanced. The aches began beneath the itching of his bandages, especially around his calves as he ran.

The exercise was good, even though he was alarmingly weak. The insects made the sand even more slippery. It made him pause for breath several times, and these pauses allowed his racked body to flood him with pain, informing him of his condition.

Odd. He was facing a wall of sand. There were no walls on Tacker's place. Parmiter was lying flat on his face. He did not even remember falling. He got up, roaches cascading off his body like sand pouring down a pole to a pile at his feet. He blundered on through the field through waves of agony.

The roaches became even more numerous the closer he got to the chasm. They were now a thick, writhing carpet covering his feet up to his kneecaps. He had to wade through the rustle of clicks of the lost, gorging bodies the way he waded through water. Most of the ground around here was just a coating of light ash from burned crops.

Interesting problem. So many of them eating garbage would wipe out their own food supply in minutes. He pondered this for a few minutes before realizing he was lying on his face again on the verge of consciousness. Theories were merging into dreamy fantasies, and only the questing, angry buzz of roaches half burying him, galvanized him to his feet.

He gasped as the separate stings of his burns flowed into rivers of pain.

"Wall!" he gasped at the roaches. "Wall!"

Jordy Harris' farm glowed a dull horizon-lining red, and Parmiter heard men shouting down that way.

The roaches kept pouring into the field from the surrounding countryside, burning every standing structure—chicken coops, curing sheds, houses, and then themselves as their numbers swelled to surging hillocks. Through the mass of bodies Parmiter felt his feet hit concrete, its hardness as shocking as its sudden appearance. He stopped running and pain engulfed him, then receded as his mind ticked over the problem.

Before concreting it, Tacker had pushed sand and fill into the chasm all the way to the top. The rock fault through which the insects had come was probably a hundred or so feet down. They would have to burrow down through the sand, just as they had burrowed up to daylight, until they found the fault themselves. They would have to. He could do nothing more.

Once he had envisioned the problem, the mere setting of the dynamite was something Parmiter did not even remember. His imagination about how it was done coincided perfectly with reality. His body strung the fuses; his mouth swiftly murmured, "Wall, wall! It's me, I'm here, I'm helping you. . . ."

Something white appeared on the ground beneath the glow of the fires. Concrete. The roaches were clearing away from the chasm. Parmiter looked behind him as he kneeled to set the fuses. The roaches had become still. A narrow path of sand led back from the chasm.

Parmiter feverishly continued setting fuses and stuffing dynamite around the edges of the chasm. "It's me. It's me!" he whispered.

The tide of insects abated from around him. The chirps died down across the fields. The concrete was now completely uncovered. Antennae went still and waited. Parmiter felt the massive millions of eyes, behind which were millions of poised watching brains like sharp needles aimed at him from the darkness. Suddenly he was out of dynamite. He considered for some time what to do next. Ah! Light it.

Parmiter lit the fuses. The fire blasted into his eyes, dazzling him. He watched them burn like angry, spitting snakes crawling to the edges of the chasm. The blue-white glare lit up the surrounding ground. Outside the concrete no sand was visible except for his path, only roaches buzzing in anticipation.

Parmiter turned and walked rapidly down the sandy path. The roaches closed ranks behind him, sealing the way to the chasm. Then he broke into a run. Metbaum's car burned with a smoky dirty blaze. He hoped Metbaum was not in there, but he was too far gone to feel anything passionately.

Parmiter felt the wave build in him. He started running. He had not killed Metbaum, had he? No, not that—he could not take anymore. As the wave rose, slowly blanking out the night, Parmiter ran faster and faster, inhibitions flying from his legs. The wave closed over him. And then a sheet of God's wrath split the night into timid fragments behind him.

Each dynamite bundle went off separately with concatenation after concatenation ringing like celestial bell strokes across the fields. The explosions gouged out chunks of sand, earth, and concrete, and hurled them to the heavens.

The concussions drove Parmiter to his knees, sinking him down closer into the soft layer of insects.

The ripples of thunder ceased leaping toward the tormented horizons. Parmiter frantically tried to clear an opening through the roaches down to the sand. "It's me, it's me," he said repeatedly.

Boulders began raining down around him, but Parmiter still did not move. Gripped by the delirium and imprisoned in the great silver wave, his hands pushed at the bodies, looking for some blank sand, looking for a sign. He felt an undertow of movement as the roaches surged toward the chasm. Lights appeared around the corner of the highway. A spot of sand appeared beneath the restless movement. The sand enlarged until he could see ridges on its surface. The glare from the lights cast shadows revealing a tracing in the sand. A word. GOODBYE.

Epilogue

WHEN the sun rose, the roaches still covered Montgomery County. They were stacked three deep in Tacker's farm pastures like locusts which had been pinned in a box canyon. As their numbers grew in Candor, the fires abated throughout the rest of the state, which lead Wiley King to conclude that the bugs were migrating to the chasm.

Beginning the next morning and continuing through the remainder of the week, aerial spray planes dive-bombed them with endrin and parathion bombs, destroying them in such numbers that the land seemed to become brown when seen from a plane.

That night Metbaum's delirious figure staggered out of the night, covered with roaches, through the doorway to the Montgomery Junior High School, where many of the families had found temporary quarters. He was driven back to Raleigh in an ambulance.

Linden met him in the hospital, where he was treated for shock and put to sleep with sedatives. He remained delirious for a week. Linden sat up with him, just as Metbaum had sat up with Parmiter before him.

By the end of the week trucks were able to drive over Route 1 without being inundated with insects. Henry Tacker moved back to his ruined house and decided to sell his land and be rid of his problems once and for all.

The police found Metbaum's burned car on the road in front of Tacker's home as well as chunks of concrete spread all over

Tacker's north pasture land. They traced the dynamite purchases to Metbaum, and they traced Parmiter's stay to the afternoon they had spent with Miss Parker. They had no trouble deducing that Metbaum had sneaked Parmiter away from the hospital down to Candor for the purpose of dynamiting the chasm.

No crime was committed; indeed, destroying the *parmiteras* was considered a service to humanity. They asked Linden how Parmiter had known that blowing the chasm had been the correct move. "That depends on what Metbaum tells us."

Linden was stating a question that baffled them all. Parmiter had disappeared.

Metbaum finally woke up. But owing to shock he had amnesia for a month, characterized by his tearing with his fingers at his bandaged arms and screaming that the bugs were going to get him. On that basis the doctors decided his condition was not permanent. He was moved to the psychiatric ward.

Wiley King collected samples of the new generation of roaches that appeared over the sandhills. They had lost their aggregation characteristics and no longer appeared in colonies. The hard cerci disappeared, so they could no longer make fire. They could still chirp and some of them were still rather large, but the bacteria deteriorated after several generations to a few enzymes and phosphates.

King did stumble across two large creatures resembling the standard *Gromphadorhina portentosa*. The creatures copulated with lack of interest and died in one of his glass cases without producing offspring.

He wrote a piece saying that in the end he believed the *parmiteras* were truly gone, their only trace a new species of pest inhabiting only the United States and perfectly harmless except to squeamish housewives who found them in the kitchen.

Parmiter's picture appeared in several newspapers along with a brief biography. He was considered a great scientist and humanitarian who had given his life to destroy the roaches. None of the papers mentioned the fact that his body was still missing.

One day Linden walked into Metbaum's hospital room. The boy was sitting up in bed, surrounded by nurses. "I know you! You're Max Linden!" he reported cheerfully.

Linden asked the nurses to go, and sat down next to Metbaum's bed. "Yes. I'm Max Linden. And we're alone now."

It had been almost exactly one month to the day since the second plague had ended.

After Metbaum had finished, Linden tapped his foot on the floor and did a lot of spectacle polishing. "Do you think it was true?" he asked Metbaum.

Metbaum carefully said, "I'm certain he had extensive insights into their habits. He knew they would return underground."

"Migratory drive," snapped Linden. "It was becoming apparent to everybody that they were congregating en masse in Montgomery County."

"In that case, I guess you'll have to ask him."

"He's gone." Linden stood up and walked over to the window where he could see Bainboro in the distance. The town was a bit cleaner now but still unbuilt. "Under the circumstances, it's not surprising."

"Well, he said if he failed to destroy the bugs, his name would be mud."

"Nobody knew for sure he had bred them, Metbaum, until just now. Until you told me. No, I don't see how he got out of there alive."

"If the bugs recognized him, they . . ."

"Let me ask you again, Metbaum. Did you ever actually see them communicate?"

"No, but Jamis . . ."

"Jamis is dead. See the problem? Parmiter told only you about this. There is reason to believe that he was unbalanced during these past weeks. Pulling out the phone plug and all that. Very irregular working habits. The school was seriously thinking of not renewing his contract in the fall. No, I think there's no question he died down there."

189

Metbaum said, "He could have gotten over to that other farm. I made it out okay. Besides you don't think he'd come back here, do you?"

Linden seemed to become irritated by Metbaum's objections. He waved his protests away and said, "The question at the moment is you. What are you going to be doing with yourself now that he's gone? Would you like to work at the Smithsonian this summer with me? We're shorthanded as usual. . . ."

Henry Tacker worked until eight thirty that night, loading small burned pieces of pottery and cookingware that had been the only things to survive the fire.

The station wagon was packed with donated clothes and bedding. Ruth sat in the front seat, chin resting on her hand looking out across the north pasture. Neither of them said much to each other. They had spent the week being partied and patted by neighbors. Henry's brother lived in High Point. He had promised to help him find work—delivery or labor or carpentry or anything. They would make it somehow.

As Henry closed the door and inserted the key in the ignition, Ruth grabbed his arm. "Henry! Hear that?"

Henry listened. Above the cricket sounds came the high thin wail of a child screaming.

Henry climbed out of the car and looked out into the darkness. A tiny shadow moved in the greater shadow of the field. Presently it resolved itself into Herman Harris' running figure. He was crying and headed straight for them.

Henry and Ruth looked at each other. "That damned boy better not have got burned again, I swan." Choking and sobbing, Herman rushed up to the station wagon, grabbing for Henry's hand.

"What happened, Herman? What's the matter?"

"A man . . . Mr. Tacker. . . ."

"You been playing out there in that pit again?"

"There's a man out . . . there, Mr. Tacker. . . ."

"What kind of man, Herman?"

Herman's eyes were white, staring and haunted. "I seen him before. I seen him at our place. . . . He don't walk, Mr. Tacker

. . . he just floats sort of over the ground. He's always lookin' at the ground. . . ."

Henry said to Ruth, "I told Jordy he shouldn't let Herman look at all them Japanese movies on the TV. Herman, you get on back home. . . ."

Herman could not stop. He made movements with his hands to describe the apparition. "He's covered with all these bugs! . . . He lives in the big hole out there . . . I ain't the only one to see him, Mr. Tacker. . . . He looked at me. . . . He's that teacher. . . ."

"Get in the goddamn car, Herman, or I'll beat the shit out of you for talk like that. . . ."

Herman started crying again.

"What's the matter?"

"My . . . momma . . . said swearin's . . . bad, Mr. Tacker."

Tacker drove Herman directly to Jordy's house and left him off. Then he and Ruth drove away from their home, from Candor and Montgomery County, to a place where they would be big and decisive, live a smaller, more manageable existence, without feeling the weight of the heavens that the Reverend Kern Speece so enthusiastically embraced.